Starlight's
Cou...

In this exciting sequel, bo.. ...iranda and her beloved horse must have courage and loyalty to overcome the obstacles they encounter. The action is non-stop in this fast paced adventure with a genuine villain. Either story can be read alone, but as a series, it is outstanding for its forceful plot and characters whom you will love. Great contemporary horse stories are hard to find.... Miranda and Starlight's adventures will please any horse lover and encourage their interest in reading.
— *Beverly J. Rowe, MyShelf.com reviewer*

Starlight's Courage

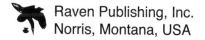

Janet Muirhead Hill

Illustrated by Pat Lehmkuhl

Raven Publishing, Inc.
Norris, Montana, USA

Starlight's Courage **Revised Edition**
© 2007 by Janet Muirhead Hill

Published by: Raven Publishing, Inc.
PO Box 2866, Norris, Montana 59745
www.ravenpublishing.net

Cover art and illustrations copyright © 2002, 2007 by Pat Lehmkuhl
Printed in the United States of America

Library of Congress Cataloging-in-Publication Data

Hill, Janet Muirhead.
  Starlight's courage / Janet Muirhead Hill ; illustrated by Pat Lehmkuhl. -- Rev. ed.
       p. cm.
  Summary: Ten-year-old Miranda Steven's adventures with the injured two-year-old stallion, Starlight, continue as she and the horse are both called upon to exhibit loyalty, courage, and endurance when a madman seeks revenge against the two of them.
  ISBN 0-9772525-4-X (pbk. : alk. paper)
  [1. Horsemanship--Fiction. 2. Horses--Fiction. 3. Schools--Fiction. 4. Friendship--Fiction.] I. Lehmkuhl, Pat, ill. II. Title.
  PZ7.H552813Sc 2007
  [Fic]--dc22
                                        2006039008

In loving memory of my father

Allen Thomas Muirhead

who shared his love, respect, and appreciation
for horses with his children

Chapter One

The heavy Montana sky threatened snow at any moment, and the driving October wind stung Miranda Stevens's face and hands. She sat alone on the swings missing her best friend, Laurie Langley. Laurie was sick again. The final recess was just beginning. Lisa and Stephanie, hands cupped around their mouths threw sidelong glances her way as they giggled and gasped. Miranda didn't know what sort of meanness they were up to, but it was obvious that she was the object of their jokes.

"Miranda, do I ever have a surprise for you!" boomed Christopher Bergman's voice.

"Don't scare me like that, Chris," Miranda shouted, spinning around to find his pale blue eyes so close she had to lean back to see them. "What surprise?"

"Can't tell you yet," Chris said, grinning, "But I know you'll like it."

"How do you know?" Miranda snapped, pushing away from him. "If you won't tell me, why bring it up?"

Amazed at how fast he sparked her anger, she fought for control, but she felt like punching his pudgy face. At moments like this he seemed more like an enemy than the close friend he had become.

Chris straddled the swing next to hers and leaned close. "I know you better than you think I do. I said it to try to cheer you up. You look like you just lost your best friend."

"Well, it didn't cheer me up, so just leave me alone."

"Oooh, aren't they a darling couple, Lisa?" taunted Stephanie as she, Lisa, Kimberly, and Tammy swaggered up. "I bet they get married someday, don't you?"

"I bet so, too. Just think what kind of children they'll have. Will they be fat and redheaded like Chris or skinny and mousy like Miranda?" asked Lisa.

"Buzz off, you jerks!" Miranda shouted, jumping out of her swing. "I wouldn't marry Chris if he were the last boy on earth. I don't even like him. If you don't stop saying I do, I'll punch your dirty mouth."

"Oh, we hit a sore spot, huh?" Stephanie giggled as Lisa drew back in fright.

"You don't dare hit me, Miranda," Lisa snarled. "You get in any more fights, and you'll be suspended."

"Look what you've done, Miranda," gloated Kimberly. "You made your boyfriend cry."

Miranda looked sharply at Christopher. A tear slid over his freckled cheek.

"She didn't make me cry!" he shouted. "I don't like her, either. Why should I? She has the meanest temper of any girl I know."

He jumped from the swing and stomped off. A strange feeling welled up in Miranda's chest. Remembering how she felt all the times she had been ignored and insulted since she came to Country View School, it shocked her that she could hurt someone else's feelings in the same way. The day suddenly seemed darker and lonelier than ever.

"You going to Shady Hills?" Miranda asked Chris when school let out, and kids began getting on the buses.

"Yeah," Chris muttered, brushing past her.

"Well, do you mind if I come?"

"Do what you want."

Miranda sat in the back seat of Bergman's mini-van, staring at the back of Christopher's carrot-colored hair. A thick blanket of tension dampened all conversation, and they rode to Shady Hills in silence. Miranda's anger had long since fled, leaving her with regret. As she thought about the good times she and Chris had enjoyed, she had to admit she really liked him. Not just because he had a horse. Not just because she got a free ride with his mother to visit her beloved Starlight. But because he was, underneath his mocking grin or taunting sarcasm, a sensitive, caring person. His obnoxious teasing and rude remarks hid his true character from most people, but he had given her the chance to really know him.

His bullying had turned to friendliness when he asked her to help him with Queen, the thoroughbred mare his parents had bought for him. It was the beginning of a shaky friendship between Miranda and Chris, born of shared confidences and unusual adventures. Miranda shook her head sadly at how her anger at the girls in her class had spoiled it all. She decided to apologize as soon as they got to Shady Hills.

When the Bergman's mini-van pulled away, she followed Chris as he tromped toward Queen's stall.

"Chris," she called, but he didn't even slow down. "Chris, wait. I want to talk to you."

He veered into the tack shed and slammed the door.

"Fine," she said to the closed door. "Go ahead and hold a grudge. Who needs you anyway?"

An eager neigh greeted Miranda as she headed toward Starlight's stall. The sound put a spring in her step, and she laughed at Starlight's bobbing head and the scraping of his hoof against his dutch door. She skipped to the two-year-old stallion as he stretched his neck out to her.

She forgot about Chris as she examined Starlight's wounds. They seemed to be healing, but progress was slow. Less than two months ago, Cash Taylor, Starlight's owner, had left orders to have him put out of his misery because the cuts were so deep that the colt's prospects were dim. Now he was gaining weight and strength. Miranda gently applied more salve and redressed each wound before leading him out of the stall into his paddock.

"I think you're getting better. You're not limping quite as much," she observed.

But tears stung her eyes as she remembered how he used to be. From the first moment she saw him, she had proclaimed him the most beautiful horse in the world and wished with all her heart that he could be hers. His eyes sparkled with life. His sleek black body glistened like the blue-black feathers of a raven. Beneath his silky forelock was a four-pointed star. It was the reason she named him Starlight. His registered name, Sir Jet Propelled Cadillac, just didn't fit his proud and wild demeanor. Sadly, she hadn't seen that spirit since the day she had trespassed by coming with Chris, secretly climbed on Starlight's back, and let him escape from his paddock.

The memory hit her stomach like a ball of ice. She couldn't erase the vision of the accident from her mind. She had seen the terror in his eyes as he fought the ever-tightening barbed wire that held him prostrate in the muddy bog.

"I'll make it up to you somehow," Miranda whispered. "I love you, and I'll never forget how much I owe you."

"How's Sir Jet today?" asked a voice behind her.

"Oh, hi, Mr. Taylor, I think he's better. I just changed the bandage on his pastern and walked him a little. You don't think that will hurt him, do you?"

"Don't overdo it. That cut is right where he bends it with every step he takes. Walking keeps it open. See? It's bleeding again."

Miranda looked at the white wrap she had just put around his right hind leg, just above the hoof. It was already bright red.

"How can we get it to heal without getting all stiff?" Miranda asked. "I sure don't want to hurt him."

"Oh, it'll be stiff, all right. I told you he'd never make a racehorse after that injury. I'm afraid he's good for nothing but a pet, so just keep him comfortable."

The old man's voice had an edge that cut like a knife into Miranda's already dejected mood. As Mr. Taylor strode away, Miranda was sure he blamed her for the loss of his finest prospect. And why not? She blamed herself.

Lost in reverie, Miranda brushed Starlight until his coat gleamed. "Mr. Taylor's so unpredictable, I never know what he'll do next or what kind of mood he'll be in. I used to think he was a total grouch, but sometimes he can be nice," she murmured to Starlight. "He scared me half to death the first time I saw him. If it hadn't been for you, I might have quit coming here." Her voice trailed off, and

she busied herself cleaning Starlight's stall, watering and feeding him. When she finished, she picked up the brush again. He stood with his eyes half closed as if enjoying each stroke of the brush. "Maybe you'd be better off if I had obeyed Mr. Taylor and stayed off his land. You'd be running free. Well maybe not free. They'd be training you for the racetrack. But you'd be…" She put her arms around his neck, pressed against his scarred chest and dreamed of better days ahead.

The crunch of Mrs. Bergman's mini-van in the gravel interrupted her reverie, and she thought of Chris. She bade Starlight goodbye and hurried to Queen's stall. "Can I help you, Chris?" Her agreement with Chris was that she help him with his horse. She always had until today.

"I don't need your help. Tell Mom I'll be through in a minute," Chris growled. "I just need to feed and water her."

"I'll get the hay, while you run the water," Miranda offered, eager to make amends.

"I said I don't need your help!"

His eyes were red, and his anger was obvious.

"I'm sorry, Chris. I didn't mean what I said today. Honest. I was just in a bad mood."

"Would you please go tell Mom I'm coming?"

"Fine!" Miranda turned on her heels and strode to the waiting mini-van.

The ride back to town was even gloomier than the ride to Shady Hills had been. *What happened to all the dreams I thought had come true?* Miranda wondered. Maybe she had wished for the wrong things and got them. She had told

Laurie once that there were three things she wanted more than anything else. One was a horse of her own. Well, she got to take care of Starlight as if he were hers, but her joy about that was mixed with guilt. His injuries had made him dependent on her. Otherwise, he probably wouldn't let her get near him. What a sacrifice for her wish to come true!

Her second wish was for friends; for a best friend. Laurie Langley was the answer to that, but she seemed to be sick a lot, which meant she wasn't there when Miranda needed her. Surprisingly, chubby, red-haired, freckled, and often rude Christopher Bergman had become a friend, too—until today.

Her third wish was to have a "regular" family, like all the other kids at her school, who lived with both parents. Instead, Miranda lived with her grandparents, John and Kathy Greene. She loved them very much. They were as good to her as any regular parents could be, but she missed her Mom. Yet, she'd turned down the chance to go live with her. At times like this, Miranda wished she'd gone.

She didn't know her father. He'd disappeared from her life before she was born. When in a low mood, like today, she imagined him coming for her. She pictured him tall, strong, and handsome with a bright smile as he lifted her into his arms. Miranda shook her head. She was always wishing and dreaming. She trudged to the house after Mrs. Bergman dropped her off. Grandma met her at the door with the phone.

"For you, Sweetie," Grandma said, "your mother."

Chapter Two

Miranda stretched and smiled, feeling as sunny as the light that slanted through her window. The new day had dawned as crisp and clear as her mood. Her talk with Mom the night before had turned her world right-side-up again. If she accomplished nothing else today, she would take her mother's advice and make up with Christopher. Staring into the bathroom mirror, she studied the ever changing, gray-green eyes and the freckles that marched across her slender nose. Her long, dark blonde hair (dishwater blonde, Great Aunt Francine called it) framed her oval face.

"It seems like I'm a different person every day," Miranda mused to her reflection. "Yesterday, I was the saddest person on earth, until I talked to Mom. She really listened to me this time. She didn't lecture me when I told her what I said to Chris. She did the same thing to a kid when she was in school, but she never apologized, and she's sorry she didn't. That's why I'm going to make up with Chris before it's too late. She laughed when I told her I call those snobs in my class the Magnificent Four."

She frowned as she leaned closer. "Why did Lisa call me mousey? I don't look like a mouse. I suppose it's because I don't have hair so blonde it's almost white like she does. But I'm not going to let her spoil my day."

"Miranda, the bus will be here in five minutes. Are you ready?" called Grandma from the kitchen.

Miranda tied back her hair, grabbed her books and jacket, and sped out the door.

"Whoa! Where's my hug?" Grandma called after her.

Miranda ran back, smiling.

"Bye, Gram. I love you," she said as she hugged her grandmother.

"Have a good day, Sweetie."

"I plan to. I'm going to Shady Hills with Chris again, if he'll let me. Okay, Grandma?"

"I suppose, but let me know."

Laurie was sitting at her desk, dabbing at her nose with a tissue, when Miranda came in.

"Hi, Laurie! I missed you yesterday. Are you feeling better?" She didn't think Laurie looked very well.

"I still have a little cough, but I couldn't stand to stay in bed another day. I was sick all weekend."

Christopher slid into his seat across from Miranda just as the bell rang. "Chris, I gotta talk to you at recess, okay?" Miranda whispered.

He made a huffing sound and put a book in front of his face. He avoided Miranda and Laurie during morning recess. At lunch, when Miranda put her tray beside his, he got up and moved to a different table.

"What's the matter with him?" asked Laurie. "He must think I have the plague or something. Maybe I should've stayed home until I was better."

"It isn't you," Miranda said. "The Magnificent Four were making a big deal about Chris and me talking. I got mad and said I didn't like him. He's still mad at me."

Stephanie, Lisa, Kimberly, and Tammy were on the swings when Miranda and Laurie went to the playground after lunch. "Great! They know we always sit in the swings. That's the only reason they're there," Miranda grumbled.

"Well, let them. If we don't say anything, they won't have the satisfaction of making us mad," Laurie said, leading the way to the teeter-totters. They sat on the bar between them to talk as best friends do.

"Uh, oh. Here come the Magnificents. They are determined to bug us," Miranda said.

"Want to watch the game with us and cheer the guys on?" asked Lisa, pointing at boys playing tag football.

"We're not really interested in football; thanks, anyway," said Laurie.

"Oh, I forgot. You are too good to associate with us. Too bad, 'cause this is your last chance. Are you sure you don't want to come help us boo the fat boy, Miranda? Or were you lying about not liking him?" Stephanie taunted.

"Yes, Stephanie, I was lying. I do like Chris. He's a heck of a lot nicer than you four ever thought of being. And don't call him fat boy!"

"Aha!" Lisa shouted. "Listen up everyone. Miranda loves Christopher Bergman. She's going to beat me up if I call him 'fat boy' again."

Miranda's face burned as the boys stopped playing and stared at her.

"Miranda loves the fat boy. Miranda loves the fat boy," chanted Lisa. Stephanie and Tammy chimed in.

Miranda clenched her fists and shouted, "Shut your mouth, Lisa. You don't know anything about friends."

Lisa kissed the back of her hand with loud smacking and slurping and said, "This is what Miranda wants to do to Chris."

When Miranda started toward her, Lisa climbed the ladder to the top of the slide. Lisa led her friends in a chant for all to hear, "Miranda and the fat boy, sitting in a tree, K-I-S-S-I-N-G."

Miranda watched the boys shake their heads and turn back to their game as she seethed with anger. She wanted revenge and stomped toward Kimberly, who was still on the ground. But a glance at Christophers' solemn, red face changed her mind. She walked up the teeter totter to it's fulcrum, put her two index fingers between her lips, and emitted a loud, shrill whistle. The playground became silent and every eye was on her.

"I DO like Chris!" she yelled as everyone listened. She gulped and continued. "Yesterday I told Lisa and Stephanie I didn't like Christopher Bergman. That was a lie. He's one of my best friends. That doesn't mean we are in love like they said. It just means, well, when things get rough we stand up for each other. I'm sorry I said I hate him. I don't!"

For a long moment, Chris stood staring at her as if he were petrified. She was afraid she'd only embarrassed him. Then he strode toward her.

"Thanks, Miranda. Truce?"

She smiled in relief and nodded.

"Let's shake on it then." He held out his right hand. She took it and jumped down.

"One thing, though," Miranda said. "I reserve the right to get mad at you. I can't promise not to punch you when you drive me crazy. But I'll fight anyone who calls you names."

"That's okay. Punch me all you want. What are friends for, anyway?"

When Miranda and Laurie got to the playground for the last recess, Chris was saving the swings for them.

"I have something to ask you," he said. "My parents signed me up to ride Queen in four events in the Winter Fair. I said I couldn't learn it all, both English and Western. Dad finally said if I work on the English events, I can ask you two to ride in the western ones.

"Really? You know we would," Miranda said.

"Of course, I'll have to ask my parents," Laurie said.

"Well there's one stipulation. Mom's afraid if you get hurt, your parents would sue her, so Dad said they would have to sign a waiver if you ride."

"I think Grandma and Grandpa would do that. Just think, we can show the Magnificent Four they aren't the only ones who're good with horses."

She had listened to the other girls in her class gloat endlessly about the horse show at the Gallatin County Winter Fair. Each year they hauled their horses to the Bozeman fairgrounds. They stayed in a hotel and ate in fancy restaurants every night. They loved to brag about the ribbons they won.

"I hope Grandma and Grandpa will let me go," Miranda said. "They can never leave their milk cows. But I'm sure they'd sign a waiver if we can figure out a way for me to get there."

"I bet I can talk my mom into taking us both," said Laurie excitedly. "I'll ask as soon as I get home."

Chris and Miranda saddled Queen at the hitching rail in front of the tack shed. As they tightened the girth, a four-wheel-drive pickup skidded to a stop in a cloud of dust. A tall, lean young man stepped out and strode over to Chris with his hand extended.

"Hi, you must be Christopher. I'm Adam Barber. Your dad hired me to give you some riding tips."

"Oh, uh, thanks," Chris stammered.

"And this is Queen," Miranda said, patting the sorrel mare.

"What a beauty," whistled Adam. "This should be fun. Let's get started."

He took the reins from Miranda without giving her a second glance. His brown eyes surveyed the graceful lines of the tall thoroughbred. Miranda stood for a moment, staring at the broad shoulders and wavy black hair of the riding instructor as he ran his hands down the mare's legs. Finally, she fled to Starlight's stall.

Miranda gasped when she saw Starlight lying down, his nose resting on the floor. She sighed in relief when he scrambled to his feet. "I thought you were sick," she said.

He pressed his soft muzzle into her shoulder, and she ran her hands over his eyes and down his face. She felt his nose for a sign of fever but found none.

"I love you, Starlight. It doesn't matter if the whole world ignores me, as long as you're happy to see me."

She gently removed the soiled bandages from Starlight's back leg. She cleaned the wound with warm, soapy water and dabbed it gently with a soft towel. Starlight didn't flinch as she sprayed some blue-violet antiseptic into the deep gash above his hoof. She wrapped it with fresh bandages. She sprayed some more of the purple medicine over the stitched cuts on his left shoulder. The veterinarian said they didn't need bandages anymore. She smoothed a greasy salve over shallower gashes which had healed to mere scabs.

Leading him out the back door of his stable into the paddock, Miranda watched him closely. His ears pointed forward, and his eyes seemed to brighten as he snorted. Because of his excitement to be outdoors, she decided to give him some freedom. She snapped the lead rope off the halter instead of tying him to the fence. He limped to the far end of the long paddock. Remembering Mr. Taylor's warning, she hurried to clean the stall so she could put him back inside. After spreading fresh shavings, she headed toward Starlight. An angry voice stopped her.

"What the devil is that horse doing in the paddock?"

"I, I..." Miranda's face burned and her heart pounded as she met Mr. Taylor's eyes. "I didn't think he'd go anywhere. I just wanted to let him enjoy the fresh air."

"I tell you not to overdo the exercise, and you turn him loose to wreak havoc on his injuries. You better start thinking or give up trying to take care of that horse," Mr. Taylor roared. "Now get him in here, and don't let him run loose again until he's healed!"

Miranda obeyed as tears flooded her eyes. The fresh bandage was soaked again, and Starlight seemed to be in pain as he limped into the stall. Mr. Taylor entered with fresh bandages and medicine.

"Get out of here," he shouted. "I'll take care of him."

Miranda opened her mouth but couldn't force a word past the lump in her throat. Tears ran down her cheeks as she backed through the stable door into the paddock. Turning, she ran into the lane that led to the pasture. She followed the well-worn bridle path until it curved back toward the stables.

Leaving the path, she climbed a hill above the river. She found a game trail switching back and forth up the steep incline into a wooded area. Rounding a corner beneath an outcropping of rocks, she stopped to stare. A gaping hole loomed above her. She climbed the last few feet to the mouth of a huge cave.

Chapter Three

The Wednesday morning air was crisp and cold. The two inches of snow that had fallen the night before intensified the sun's brilliance. Miranda made shadow pictures on the pages of her history book as the monotone voice of one of her classmate's droned in the background. She couldn't get Mr. Taylor's stinging rebuke out of her mind.

He doesn't think I can take care of Starlight. Or maybe he's sorry he promised not to kill him, since it's taking so long for him to heal. What if he changes his mind? Miranda began to make a plan to save Starlight in case Mr. Taylor showed any sign that he was thinking of getting rid of him. She thought of the cave she had explored yesterday. The room near the entrance was big enough for her and Starlight to hide in. It was hidden from the trail, the ranch headquarters, or anyone who might be riding on the bridle path. She hadn't had time to explore all the passages, but there was at least one big enough to get Starlight out of sight from the opening.

"Miranda! I asked you to read next." The teacher's voice brought Miranda abruptly back to the classroom.

"Uhmm, I'm sorry," Miranda said, staring at her book with no idea where the last reader had left off.

Laurie whispered, "Top of page eighty-nine." Miranda turned two pages and began where Laurie's finger marked a new section.

By noon, Laurie was feeling terrible again. After testing her temperature with the back of her hand, Mrs. Penrose called her mother. Mrs. Langley, with her blonde hair tied into a messy pony-tail and wearing a paint spattered shirt, came to take Laurie home. Miranda went to the lunch room alone and took her tray to a table by the window where she could see the snow-covered peaks. Her mind returned to the cave and Starlight.

"What's the matter, Miranda? Did your boyfriend dump you?" Miranda ignored Stephanie's taunting voice.

"Really, Miranda, you don't have to be all by yourself," Lisa said, sitting next to her. "If you dumped your little mulatto friend and stayed away from Creepy Chris, you could be our friend."

Miranda frowned as she looked across the table to see that all four of the Magnificents had joined her. She had never heard the word mulatto and had no idea what it meant, but she wasn't about to tell them that.

"Who asked you to sit here? I was here first, and I don't want company," Miranda said.

"Well, for your information, you don't own this table," Tammy retorted.

"We're serious," Kimberly said. "We talked it over, and we all agree. We decided to let you join our riding club. Since you don't have a horse of your own, I'll let you ride one of mine on the days we go out together."

As if she has dozens, Miranda thought. "Why are you asking me now? Do you expect me to turn on my friends, so I can ride one of your precious horses? Forget it."

"You don't get it, do you?" Stephanie sneered. "You could be popular if you quit hanging out with losers. Josh told me he likes you, but he isn't going to be your boyfriend if you keep hanging out with Chris and Laurie."

"I don't care what Josh thinks. I've got more important things to worry about than having a boyfriend."

"Fine. You'll be sorry, though," Stephanie said. "Just don't forget we warned you."

Most of the snow had melted by the time Miranda and Chris arrived at Shady Hills. She ran to check on Starlight, half-afraid he wouldn't be there. As she approached his stall, he greeted her enthusiastically with nodding head and a deep-throated rumble. Miranda brought some rolled oats with molasses and let him eat them from her hand. She noticed that he had a new kind of wrap on his pastern. She knelt to inspect it closely. It was hard and tight and looked quite clean.

"I had Doc put that on him this morning," said Cash Taylor.

Miranda jumped to her feet to meet the pale blue eyes beneath the bushy, white eyebrows, as the old man leaned on the lower half of the dutch door.

"Sorry I was a little gruff yesterday. I've been under a bit of a strain lately. That wrap will support his ankle better and keep the wound from breaking open when he walks. If that doesn't work, we'll put it in a plaster cast. Don't walk him more than you have to for a few weeks. The vet'll take care of that dressing. It won't need to be changed every day."

Miranda nodded, relaxing a little as Mr. Taylor showed his softer side again. *I'll never understand this man.*

"Oh, by the way," he added as he turned to leave. "I'll be away for a couple weeks. Flying to England tomorrow."

"England? Why?" Miranda asked, hurrying to the door. But Mr. Taylor disappeared around the corner of the stables without a backward glance.

Miranda and Chris set up obstacles to practice for the trail class at the Winter Fair. It involved things like crossing a wooden bridge, opening and closing a gate, getting something from a mailbox and hanging it on a hook on the wall, all without dismounting. For lack of a bridge, they laid some planks on the floor of the arena. At first Queen shied away from them. It took just a little coaxing for her to understand she was supposed to walk on them.

"She probably thinks we're crazy," Miranda called to Chris. "We've always asked her to jump these planks before. Now she wonders why we want her to step on them."

Miranda caught a movement out of the corner of her eye and looked up to see Adam standing near the door.

"Quite the versatile mare," he remarked. "I hope all this child's play doesn't make her forget her real business. Go get your saddle, Chris, we've got work to do."

Miranda heard the scorn in Adam's voice and wondered why he disliked her. She dismounted and took Chris's expensive western saddle off Queen's back. She stood with her back to Adam as she stroked the mare's nose and thanked her for the ride.

"Here! I'll take her," said Adam as he pulled the reins from Miranda's hands. She glared at him and started to speak. But Adam was scratching Queen's ear and talking to her. "At least they didn't put a western bridle on you. It's a wonder."

Miranda lugged the heavy saddle back to the tack room. *If Adam was a gentleman, he'd have helped me,* she thought. She stayed with Starlight the rest of the day.

When Miranda opened her locker the next morning, a sheet of paper fell to the floor. She was about to stuff it into her notebook when she realized it wasn't hers. It was a crude drawing of three people, two girls and a boy. Across the top in red crayon were the words, "The three stupids!" She seethed as she read the bold lettering beneath each picture: "Orphan," "Fat Boy," and "Nigger."

Miranda shuddered at the last inscription. It was a word she considered vulgar and unspeakable. Obviously, the boy in the middle with the red hair, round face, and big round body was meant to be Chris, and the stick figure with long stringy hair, labeled orphan was Miranda. The one with the curly, black hair must be Laurie, but she couldn't think why anyone would call her friend—that word!

She looked up to see Kimberly, Stephanie, and Tammy staring at her.

"Did you creeps do this?"

"No."

"Yeah, right. Then why are you watching me?"

"Are you calling my friends liars?" asked Lisa as she appeared from around the corner.

"What if I am?" asked Miranda.

"You'll be sorry, that's what!"

"Did you put this in my locker, Lisa?" asked Miranda holding up the drawing.

"Maybe. Pretty good picture, don't you think. It looks

just like you stupids. You are so pathetic. A fat boy, a nigger, and an orphan. Why don't your parents want you, Miranda?"

Miranda dropped the offending paper, lunged at Lisa, and hit her squarely on the mouth with her fist. Stephanie screamed, and Tammy grabbed Miranda's hair and pulled hard. Miranda dug her fingernails into Tammy's wrist until she let go. Stephanie and Lisa yanked and scratched Miranda's hands and arms. Miranda swung around to face them, lowered her head, slammed into Stephanie's abdomen. Stephanie fell down and gasped for breath.

"Get away from us, you maniac!"

"What's going on here?" shouted Mrs. Penrose. "Break it up and come with me. All of you."

"She's crazy, Mrs. Penrose!"

"She started pounding on us for no reason!"

Miranda looked for the offending picture, but Kimberly beat her to it. She snatched it up from the floor before Miranda could reach it. Mrs. Penrose caught Miranda by the arm.

"Did you start this, Miranda?"

"No, that picture started it."

"What picture?"

"The one Kimberly has in her hands."

Kimberly held out both hands and shrugged as if she didn't know what the "crazy girl" was talking about.

"I'm taking you to the office to let Mr. Alderman sort this out. I must get back to the rest of my class." Mrs. Penrose didn't let go of Miranda's arm until the five girls stood in the principal's office.

"Let's have a look at your lip, Lisa," said the teacher before she left. "It's bleeding pretty badly and swelling fast. I don't think it will need stitches, but I'll have someone bring you some ice. We'll keep an eye on it."

Mr. Alderman shook his head gravely as he asked for an explanation. The Magnificents all claimed they didn't know what got into Miranda.

"She just flew off the handle and started attacking," they said. "We just tried to defend ourselves."

"Is that right, Miranda?"

"They shouldn't be calling me and my friends names."

"No, I'm sure they shouldn't. But whatever they might have called you, it doesn't justify that type of behavior. This isn't the first time you've been caught using physical violence. There are better ways to resolve disagreements. I can't tolerate this kind of behavior in my school, so I'm suspending you for the rest of the week, Miranda. The rest of you may go back to class."

Chapter Four

"Grandma," Miranda pleaded as she closed her science book, "please let me go to Shady Hills this afternoon. I've studied hard all morning, and there's nothing else to do."

"Miranda, it's plain and simple. If you get suspended from school, which I never thought I'd see, you are also grounded at home." Grandma wiped her hands and sat down at the table across from Miranda. "It really puzzles me that you would strike your classmates. We've always preached and modeled nonviolence."

"I know," Miranda said, unable to meet Grandma's eyes. "They just made me so mad, I couldn't help it."

"Couldn't help it? Give me a break, Miranda. Your mother always 'helped it' when you kept her awake all night with your crying. Your grandpa and I have always 'helped it' when you provoked us with your lying, or worried us half to death. No one in our family has ever so much as swatted you. There are more effective ways of dealing with anger. Can't you see that?"

"Yes, I do, Gram. I don't know why I do it. I just want to hit people when they say mean things about my family or my friends."

"Well, maybe with the rest of the week to think it over, you'll come up with a better way. I'm sure you can find something else to study."

Miranda sighed and wandered to the bookshelf in the dining room. Beside it on a pedestal was a big unabridged dictionary. She thumbed through it absentmindedly. What was that word Lisa had called Chris? Malotto or something like that. After looking for it under ma, me, mi, mo, she finally found mulatto: *The first generation offspring of a European and a black.* That made no sense. *Chris? No not Chris, Laurie!* That fit with the label on the stick figure in the drawing, but why Laurie? She wasn't black. She closed the dictionary.

"May I go outside, Gram?"

"That's a good idea. You've been cooped up in the house all day."

Miranda wandered across the barnyard toward the corrals and the pasture beyond. The warm sun shone brightly on the golden yellow leaves of the aspen and cottonwood. The currant bushes were the color of a pumpkin. Some low-lying shrubs glowed bright red, and a tall bush was deep purple. It would be a perfect day to ride Queen through the river pasture at Shady Hills.

She worried about Starlight. Would he remember her when she went back to see him? Did he feel lonely and abandoned? Maybe he would get sick again. Mr. Taylor was gone, and Higgins, the groom and caretaker, wouldn't have time to more than feed and water him. Laurie had promised to look in on him every day she went with Chris, but that was little consolation. She needed to be there herself so he wouldn't forget her.

Miranda walked through the pasture, turning the cows into beautiful horses with her imagination. This was the horse ranch she and Laurie planned to own someday. Starlight, in the form of a rangy, black cow, was king. Many of the prize-winning racehorses were his offspring. Others were top of the line brood mares she had bought to breed to him, the most famous thoroughbred in the country.

One of them looked up and stared as Miranda approached. "This black and white paint, registered Shooting Star, is one of the world's finest race horses and the number one prospect for winning the next Kentucky Derby!" Miranda proclaimed with a sweeping gesture.

But the gentle milk cow only blinked. Her bovine stare and cud-chewing complacency just didn't fit Miranda's vision of a sleek and skittish racehorse.

"You're just a dumb old cow, Bessie," she said, as she scratched the Holstein between the eyes.

Miranda remembered bucket-feeding Bessie when she was a tiny calf. It was before she and Mom moved to California, so she must have been only four or five years old. Miranda always turned and ran as soon as the bucket was empty, knowing Bessie would run after her.

Might as well bring them in for milking. She rounded up the herd, tossing rocks and yelling, "Hey ya. Get on there," as she prodded them toward the barn. *No,* she thought. *No way to mistake these pokey old cows for racehorses.*

Miranda reached the barnyard just as the school bus approached. She was surprised to see the blinking lights come on as it slowed and then stopped at her driveway. When Chris and Laurie got off, she ran to meet them.

"Hi, Miranda," Laurie called. "We missed you, so we just came over. I hope your Grandma won't mind."

"She won't. Come on in. I just got back from a long walk, so I have to make sure she's not worrying."

They smelled freshly baked bread when they opened the kitchen door.

"You timed that just right," Grandma laughed, as she set a pan of hot rolls on the counter top to cool. "Take off your coats and pull up a chair."

After eating some hot rolls with butter and plum jelly, chased down with cold milk, Laurie and Miranda cleared the table. Chris buttered one more roll.

"These sure are good, Mrs. Greene," he said.

"Grandma, may we go play in the hayloft before I do my chores?" asked Miranda.

"Yes, and since you already brought the cows in, I'll feed and put the milkers together. Just be sure to gather the eggs and shut up the chickens before dark."

In the hayloft they took turns swinging from the rope that hung from the center of the rafters. They performed trapeze stunts and made forts in the bales of hay.

"When did you last see Starlight? Is he okay?"

"He's fine," Laurie replied. "We went yesterday. I can tell he misses you, though."

"Are you learning lots from your riding instructor, Chris?" Miranda asked.

"Yeah, he's great. I'm getting good at jumping. I'm not as scared as I used to be."

"Does Adam let you ride, Laurie?"

"Not usually. When he's there, he wants to work with Chris. But I was riding when he got there yesterday. He told me to take her around a couple more times so he could tell Chris what I was doing that he wanted him to do. He sure is nice."

"Hmmph," Miranda grunted. "I'm glad you think so. He isn't very nice to me. If he knows I'm alive, he must wish I wasn't."

"I don't know why, but I know the feeling. I can hardly wait for you to come back to school, Miranda," Laurie said. "The other girls in our class treat me like I have some deadly disease they could catch. I'd like to know what makes them hate me so much."

"They hate all three of us, but I don't know why. That's why I got into a fight with them. They drew a picture of us and wrote nasty names on it. Then Kimberly hid it so I couldn't prove they did it."

"I'm used to them treating me like a nobody. They always have, and I don't care," Chris claimed.

"They know how mad it makes me to be called an orphan just because I live with my grandparents. I'm not an orphan," Miranda said hotly. "And they call Chris 'fat boy' because they know that makes him mad. But Laurie, I can't figure out why they called you...uh, black, well actually they wrote"—Miranda could hardly say it—"'nigger.'"

"They did?" Laurie's face flushed and her eyes brimmed with tears. "That's so hateful."

"It's stupid, too. You aren't black."

"Well, partly. If it makes any difference to you, you'd better say so right now," Laurie said.

"It doesn't. I'd like you just the same if you were green or purple. I just didn't know."

"I knew your dad was half black because I heard my parents talking. It doesn't matter to me," said Chris.

"Oh, so you're dad is mulatto, not you" said Miranda, putting it together.

"Why did you call him that?" Laurie challenged.

"It's just a word I heard one of the Magnificents say. They were telling me not to be friends with a mulatto, and I didn't know what they were talking about. I thought it was something about Chris, until I looked it up today. I didn't mean anything bad by it. I was taught that people are people, no matter what color of skin they have."

"Well, I wish everyone in this town thought so. Dad said he's run into more prejudice here than in Cincinnati," Laurie said, her voice quivering.

"Why? What do people say?"

"The same thing Lisa, Kimberly, Stephanie, and Tammy are saying. They hear it from their parents, or they wouldn't think to say it themselves," said Laurie.

"I don't get it. Why do people care what color of skin your dad has? Tell him my grandparents aren't like that."

"Oh, he knows that. Just a few families make it hard for us. We always went to church before we came here, but we don't feel welcome in any of the three churches."

"That's terrible," Miranda exclaimed, "and so unfair."

"We came here because Dad had a job teaching math

to the high-school kids. But when we got here and they saw he was black, they suddenly didn't need him anymore. They said there was a mix up, and they'd hired someone else, but they hadn't. They used a substitute teacher for a week before the new math teacher got here."

"That stinks!" Miranda gasped. "So what does he do for a job?"

"He's a salesman for a ranch supply company. That's why he's gone so much."

After almost a week of studying and working at home, Miranda was ready to go back to school. The class was busily planning the school Halloween party and decorating their room in black and orange crepe paper streamers.

"Chris, you going to the stables after school?" Miranda asked at recess.

"Yeah. Can you come with me? I have a lesson with Adam, but then you can practice for the trail event."

"Good. I can hardly wait to get back on Queen. But I want to spend time with Starlight, too. I hope he hasn't forgotten me."

"Don't tell me you two are planning to compete in the horse show at the Winter Fair!" exclaimed Tammy from behind them.

"Butt out, Tammy," said Chris.

"We weren't talking to you. It's none or your business what we do," added Miranda.

"Well, I was just trying to save you from embarrassing yourselves. If you try to compete in any of the western classes, you don't have a chance. Stephanie and Lisa and I always take first place in the events we choose. There's at least one of us in every western horse event they have, so you might as well save your time and money."

"Don't count on winning this year," Miranda growled.

As Laurie was running to join Miranda and Chris, she ran into Tammy, who backed into her path. Tammy frowned and brushed off her shirt.

"Keep your cooties to yourself, Laurie."

Tears sprung to Laurie's eyes as she stared at Tammy in surprise.

"Don't pay any attention to her, Laurie. What she thinks doesn't matter. We wouldn't want her for a friend anyway."

Laurie shrugged as Tammy strutted away.

"You coming with us to Shady Hills, Laurie?" Chris asked.

"Can't. Dad's getting back from Boise today, and Mom's planning a welcome home surprise for him."

There was no doubt that Starlight remembered Miranda. He welcomed her with whinnying, head-bobbing, and hoof-stomping. The wounds on his chest were now only scar tissue that showed in lines of ruffled hair. The deep gashes on his shoulder were scabbed over. A thick, tight wrap still covered his right rear pastern.

"You beautiful boy, Starlight, you're getting better!" Miranda exclaimed. "I missed you so much."

Adam's pickup rumbled to a stop in front of the arena. Ignoring the handsome riding instructor, Miranda pumped clean water into Starlight's trough. She let him eat sweet feed from her hand. As she brushed him, she talked soothingly of her future plans and dreams.

When she heard Adam's pickup drive away, she gave Starlight a parting pat and hurried to the arena.

"How did it go, Chris?"

"Pretty good. I just can't seem to be as smooth as Adam wants me to be. But I think I'm getting better. At least I feel more relaxed. Are you ready to ride?"

"Sure. I'll practice in the English saddle, today," said Miranda, not wanting to lug the heavy western saddle from the tack shed and hoist it onto the tall mare. "I could even do it bareback."

"Let's see you open and close gates on her without a saddle," Chris challenged.

Miranda pulled off the light English saddle and handed it to Chris. After leading Queen to the platform, she jumped on her back. Riding bareback made her feel more a part of the horse. She had no trouble riding around the arena, putting Queen through all her paces and running some figure-eights around some barrels. She rode up to the metal gate at the end of the arena and leaned down to open it. It was harder to reach without a stirrup to lean into, but she gripped the mare's withers with her left leg as she leaned down from Queen's right side. She got the hook undone and backed the mare away, pulling the gate with her. She had to keep her hand on the top rail of the gate as she guided the mare around it and pulled it closed. It was tricky. She lost her grip on the gate and had to start over. The second time went a little better, but she didn't quite get it latched before she had to let go in order to keep from falling off. The third time was a triumph. She dropped the hook in the eye and signaled Queen to go on, not realizing that the sleeve of her jacket was caught in the hook. Queen turned away from the gate, but Miranda crashed against it as she was dragged from the horse.

"Miranda!" Chris shouted. "Are you hurt?"

"Ow!" said Miranda, pulling her feet under her and freeing her sleeve from the latch.

"Your head, Miranda. You're bleeding!"

Miranda put her hand to her temple, which hurt so bad she felt sick to her stomach. Her hand was red with blood when she pulled it away. She had to sit on the ground to keep from keeling over.

"What should I do?" Chris asked. "Don't bleed to death, Miranda!"

"It's not that bad, Chris. But maybe you'd better go call Grandma."

Chris sped out the door, and Miranda lay back on the ground, her hand on her forehead. She looked up when she felt a nudge to her shoulder. Queen seemed to be asking, "What are you doing down there?"

"Thank you, Queen. I love you," Miranda said. "Here, I'll take you back to your stable. Standing shakily with Queen for support, Miranda led her to the other end of the arena. Blood ran into her eye and dripped off her chin. At the door, everything went wavy, then black.

Chapter Five

Something wet and cold touched Miranda's forehead. She opened her eyes to see Grandma's worried face peering down at her. She looked around. She was lying on the ground near the door of the arena. Queen was gone.

"How do you feel, Sweetie?" Grandma asked.

"My head hurts. Did I pass out?'

"I'll say you did! For several minutes. I'm going to carry you to the car."

Before Miranda could reply, Grandma scooped her off the ground, lugged her to the car, and nestled her in the reclined front seat of her Subaru. Chris climbed in the back seat.

"Your Grandma said I could go with you. Here's another cold towel for your head," Chris hovered over the front seat like a mother hen.

"Okay, Chris, time to buckle up," Grandma said.

Miranda steeled herself when the doctor came at her with a tiny needle. She was determined not to wince or cry out as he injected something to deaden the area around the cut on the side of her forehead. There was a small prick and a sting as the medicine went in. But when the doctor put in ten tiny stitches, she didn't feel a thing.

"She has a concussion, so keep an eye on her," the doctor said to Grandma. "She'll probably have a splitting headache. Give her ibuprofen for pain, and call me if she doesn't feel much better by morning."

Chris was unusually quiet as they left the clinic. Though it was only a few blocks to his house, Grandma offered to drive him home.

"I hope you're going to be all right, Miranda," Chris said as he got out of the car. "I didn't mean for you to get hurt. I never do, but I keep getting you in trouble."

"What do you mean? You didn't do this," Miranda said.

"Well, I shouldn't have dared you to ride bareback," he whispered to Miranda.

"I would've ridden bareback anyway. I love to ride without a saddle. Don't worry, I'm going to be fine."

"Christopher," Grandma said gently. "No one is blaming you for this. Accidents happen. We'll just make sure there's a grown-up around from now on."

"Mom'll blame me," Chris murmured as he turned toward the house.

A few minutes later as they drove out of town, Miranda groaned, "Gram, stop the car. I have to throw up."

Miranda slept fitfully that night and through most of the next day, waking now and then to a dull headache and falling asleep again. She finally got up to join Grandma and Grandpa for supper, but didn't feel like eating much. She finished her milk with another pill for her headache and went back to bed. She slept through the second night without waking and felt refreshed the next morning.

She got up slowly, stretched, and gingerly touched her head. In the bathroom mirror, she studied her reflection. The side of her face and under her right eye was deep purple. She removed the bandage to peer at her stitches.

"It looks like a railroad track on a map," she laughed.

"You should tell the kids at school you got in a fight with Chris and he won," the girl in the mirror suggested.

"That would be interesting, but it would be a lie," Miranda mused. "I wonder what Chris would think."

Miranda didn't think it strange to talk to herself in the mirror. She'd solved many problems and made important decisions this way. She couldn't remember when she'd started it. She dressed for school and went to the kitchen where Grandma was talking on the phone.

"No one is blaming you, Julia, and Miranda will be fine. I just think it's unwise to let any of them ride without an adult nearby in case something does go wrong."

She must be talking to Chris's mom, Miranda thought. If she gets Mrs. Bergman all riled up, they won't let me ride Queen any more.

"No, we certainly aren't going to sue you.... No, we won't let you pay the doctor bill. Miranda might have fallen off even if we'd been there. I'm just saying let's take turns, you, me, and Mrs. Langley, to stay at Shady Hills while the kids ride."

When Grandma hung up, she saw Miranda. "Well, good morning! How do you feel today?"

"I feel great. I'm ready to go to school."

"Okay, but come home right after, and call me if you start feeling bad before then."

"But, Gram, I need to practice for the horse show."

"That can wait until your head has a chance to heal."

"Why? I don't ride with my head."

"Obviously," Grandma said with a smile.

"Oh, Gram, you know what I mean."

"I do. Still, you had a concussion and that's serious. From now on you're wearing a helmet when you ride. And you can't do that until your head heals."

"Oh, no, not a helmet. That would look ridiculous! I'm not in the habit of falling off. Yesterday was just a freak accident."

"Just come home today. First chance we get, we'll go to Bozeman or Butte and get a riding helmet. It can be a stylish hard hat like all the English riders wear. And I don't want you riding when there is no adult around to supervise."

"Why? I'm just as good a rider as I ever was. I don't need someone helping me."

"Not helping, just being close by in case something goes wrong—and to remind you not to try something that is obviously unsafe."

"I didn't think you'd start treating me like a baby just because I made one mistake," Miranda groaned.

"I'm treating you like a ten-year-old, Miranda. "

"What's the matter, Miranda? Can't you stay on a horse?"

jeered Stephanie as Miranda boarded the bus to go to school. "You'd better not try to ride in the horse show, if you can't even ride around the arena without falling off."

"Bug off, Stephanie. You don't know what happened." Miranda retorted.

"Oh, I heard. Everyone at school knows."
Wait until I get hold of Chris.

When Chris slid into his seat across from hers, Miranda growled at him. "Why'd you tell everyone that I fell off Queen?"

"I didn't! You should know me better than that!" Chris retorted.

"Then who did?"

"Lisa's aunt works in the clinic, so she told Lisa. You know what a big mouth Lisa has. She told everyone in school yesterday."

"Oh. Sorry I accused you."

Chris shrugged and continued, "They're saying you'll be afraid to get on a horse again."

"Ha. They wish!"

Another week went by before Grandma found time to go to Bozeman for a helmet. In the meantime, Mrs. Bergman was taking an art class every day, and Mrs. Langley came down with the flu. There was no way to go to Shady Hills, though Miranda begged her grandparents to take her.

"I won't ride or anything, so you don't have to worry about me. I have to see Starlight!"

But they were busy, too, and Miranda had to wait.

Grandma finally picked up a black riding helmet at the saddle shop in Four Corners on one of her quick trips to get supplies. On Saturday, she took Miranda, Laurie, and Chris to Shady Hills. Miranda ran to Starlight's stall.

"Come see him, Grandma."

Starlight greeted her eagerly as she pulled an apple from her pocket to reward him.

"Who are you?" asked a childish voice behind her.

Miranda whirled around to see a small boy with a pale, freckled face, topped with a mop of wavy brown hair.

"I'm Miranda. Who are you?"

"Elliot Montgomery. What are you doing here?"

"Feeding Starlight. What're you doing here?"

"His name is Sir Jet," the boy corrected. "I live here."

"You live here?"

"Yes. This is my new home."

Miranda was completely fascinated. She loved the British accent with which the boy spoke so firmly.

"Are you from England?" she asked him.

"Yes."

"Did Mr. Taylor bring you here?"

"Yes. He's my grandfather," Elliot said. "Who is she?"

"Oh, this is my grandmother, Kathy Greene."

"I'm pleased to meet you, Elliot," said Grandma, extending her hand to the child.

"You don't look like a grandmother," he said.

Chris and Laurie emerged from Queen's stall and started toward the arena. "Are you coming, Miranda?" Chris called.

"Not yet. Come here and meet someone."

Chris shook hands with Elliot and turned to go. Laurie stayed.

"I'll come watch you ride, Chris. I think the girls are going to be busy for awhile," Grandma offered.

"Okay, thanks," Chris said. "Nice to meet you, Elliot. Miranda and Laurie, don't forget you need to practice; come as soon as you can."

Elliot led Laurie and Miranda to the house where Cash Taylor sat at his roll-top desk, absorbed in paper work.

"You're back, Mr. Taylor!" Miranda exclaimed. "And you brought someone with you!"

"What happened to you?" Mr. Taylor asked.

"I had a little accident; nothing serious," Miranda said. "How was your trip to England? Must have been exciting to find a grandson!"

"I'd say it was! The best surprise of my life," Mr. Taylor said, looking at Elliot. He sighed and continued. "It was a very bitter-sweet two weeks. I suppose you want to hear about it?"

"Of course we do. Please tell us."

"Well, I got a registered letter the day I left here. It was from Cassy, my daughter in England. It had been forwarded from Texas and contained bad news. After not hearing from her in over thirty years, she wrote that she was dying."

"Oh, no!" Miranda and Laurie exclaimed together.

"Yes. Cancer. Well, I got on the first airplane out of Billings, scared I wouldn't make it in time, but I did. I had a few wonderful days with my daughter. She told me all about her life. I found out that she had been married for ten years and had a six-year-old child. Her husband left her when he found out she had cancer."

"What a jerk!" cried Miranda.

"I know. I called him worse than that. But Cassy said it hadn't been a happy marriage, and it was best that he left. The trouble was, she didn't want to leave Elliot with him. The only alternative she could think of was me. She said she'd been thinking about me a lot. She remembered when I had come to see her when she was little, and she wanted to know me before she died." Mr. Taylor paused to wipe a tear from his eye.

"What about her mother?" asked Miranda.

"She died a few years ago. It seems cancer runs in their family," Mr. Taylor said sadly.

"So she asked you to take Elliot and keep him?" asked Laurie.

"Yes, she did, and I couldn't refuse. After all those years of separation from my family, I was glad to get part of it back. He's a smart little lad, and very polite. His mother did a good job raising him. From what she told me, she didn't have much help from her husband." Mr. Taylor frowned and was quiet for a moment.

"At least I got the chance to know my daughter again," he continued. "She let me know how angry she was that I left and never came back. I tried to tell her it was because her mother insisted that I stay away. She didn't think that was a very good excuse, and I guess it wasn't." Mr. Taylor wiped his eyes and blew his nose.

The girls waited, hoping he would continue.

"I apologized and begged for forgiveness, of course,"

he went on. "I tried to let her know how much I wanted to come back; wanted her to come here. I told her about the piano I bought for her. We both cried, something I thought I'd forgotten how to do, and we both wished we could live those years over. But we made the most of the little time that was left. We talked and talked, more interested in getting to know each other than in eating or sleeping."

Again there was a long pause as Mr. Taylor dabbed at his eyes and blew his nose.

"She died with a smile on her face, holding my hand. Her last words were, 'Give my son all the love and opportunities you wanted to give me, Dad.'"

Mr. Taylor broke down and sobbed. Elliot put his arm around the old man, as the tears streamed down his face, too. Taking his grandson onto his lap, Cash Taylor held him, and they cried together. Miranda and Laurie tiptoed out as tears filled their own eyes.

Chapter Six

The cold winds had blown most of the leaves off the trees by mid-November, but Miranda was so busy she hardly noticed. She went to Shady Hills nearly every day. Grandma, Mrs. Bergman and Mrs. Langley took turns taking the children and watching them ride. Miranda and Chris complained about the supervision.

"We're not babies!" Chris said.

"We don't need to be baby-sat!" Miranda agreed.

"Just forget they're sitting there," Laurie advised. "They're usually reading a book or knitting and not really watching us anyway. It's kind of nice to know they're near if we need them."

Miranda soon realized that Laurie was right. She often forgot that one of the mothers was there as she practiced for the competition. Once in awhile, she even asked one of them for help with a cinch or advice on a maneuver. Both Grandma and Mrs. Langley knew far more about horses than Miranda had imagined.

Tammy, Kimberly, Stephanie, and Lisa continued to remind Miranda and Laurie that they didn't stand a chance at the Winter Fair. The idea of letting even one of the Magnificent Four beat them in any event was unthinkable, so practice became an obsession; more important than schoolwork or anything else. Even Miranda's time with Starlight lessened. She kept his stall clean, put medicine on his wounds, fed and watered him. But then, with a quick pat on his shoulder, she'd say good-bye and run off to work with Queen.

Miranda listened closely to Adam's instructions to Chris and watched his demonstrations. He sat tall in the saddle and could get Queen to do anything he asked. Miranda did her best to imitate his style, knowing he would never give her any personal instruction. She'd tried asking him questions, but he never seemed to hear or would answer so shortly that she was afraid to ask another. He was paid to tutor Chris, of course, but he offered Laurie pointers sometimes. Angry that he ignored her, Miranda made up her mind to win his attention by being the best rider of them all.

Miranda's Aunt Jolene and Uncle Corey, Mom's twin brother, came from Kalispell for Thanksgiving weekend. Grandma needed Miranda's help in getting the house spotlessly clean and the traditional feast prepared. It was fun to see her aunt and uncle and to play with her baby cousin, but she missed seeing Starlight and riding Queen.

"May I go to Shady Hills now?" Miranda asked after the chores were all done Saturday morning. Uncle Corey and Aunt Jolene had bundled their baby into his car seat in the back of their jeep and disappeared down the highway.

"Not unless Mrs. Bergman or Mrs. Langley will take you," Grandma said.

"The Bergmans aren't back from Billings yet, and Laurie has a bad cold again," Miranda whined. "I don't see why I can't just go see Starlight."

"I'm going with Grandpa to get a load of hay at Millers. If Mr. Taylor's at home, I guess we could drop you off there while we load hay. You may call him and see."

"There's no answer at Mr. Taylor's house," Miranda said, holding the phone. "May I try Higgins?"

When he didn't answer either, Miranda sighed and bundled up in her coat, mittens, and cap and climbed into the big truck next to Grandma. Going after hay was better than staying home alone, she decided. She brought along some books, thinking she could catch up on some reading while her grandparents loaded hay.

The Miller's haystack was on a hill where the wind blew fiercely. Miranda got out to climb up on the haystack, but her face was soon stinging from the cold, and her toes were going numb. She watched her grandfather brace against the wind as he threw the bales onto the flat bed of the truck where Grandma stacked them. Miranda climbed back into the cab of the truck. It was a relief to be out of the wind, but it wasn't much warmer. By the time her grandparents finished loading the hay, snow, driven by the wind, streaked horizontally past the windshield.

"Let's get this heater going," Grandma said, but the engine had cooled off, and only cold air blew from the vents. She turned off the blower. They drove slowly across the field as Grandpa strained to see the tracks that led to the gate. Miranda could see nothing but swirling sheets of

gauzy white snow. They finally turned onto the county road and headed toward home.

"I'm glad it's only five miles," Grandpa said after awhile. "This stuff is drifting across the road already. Turn on the defroster, Kathy."

The heater was beginning to feel warm on Miranda's legs, but her toes were still painfully cold. She watched Grandma switch the heater from vent to defrost.

"Whoa!" Grandpa yelled, stepping on the brake. He rolled down his window and thrust his head out into the icy wind as the truck slid sideways and came to a stop.

"What happened?" Miranda yelped as the cold air flooded the cab.

"Sorry, I knew better than that," Grandpa said as he got out to survey their situation. Grandma rolled the driver's side window up again.

"Why did it do that?" asked Miranda. She stared at the windshield which was now white instead of transparent.

"The glass was still very cold, the hot air condensed and froze on the cold windshield. We both should have known better."

"Well," Grandpa said, climbing back in and shutting the door quickly. "I wasn't expecting the storm to roll in this fast. We may get a lot more snow before this is over. Now, to get this rig back on the road."

"We're not on the road?" Miranda asked.

"No, just off the shoulder, but the ditch isn't very deep. I think if I can get it rolling, it'll go. We have plenty of weight for traction!"

He was scraping the ice off the inside of the windshield and the defroster was gradually warming it up. He cleared a peephole in the thick frost.

"I can see the tops of some grass to mark the edge of the road," he said. "Hang on, we're going for it."

At first the truck wouldn't go forward, so he eased it backward. Then he went forward a little way before it stopped again. After rocking it back and forth, a little farther each time, Grandpa finally had it back on the road and moving. Miranda let out a deep sigh and only then realized that she'd been holding her breath.

"What's this?" Grandpa stepped on the brake pedal.

The truck began to skid. Grandpa let off the brakes and tapped them repeatedly until the truck came to a stop.

"What's the matter, Grandpa?" Miranda asked as she tried to scrape ice off the side window with her mitten.

But Grandpa was already out the door.

"It looked like a car in the ditch back there," Grandma explained.

The passenger's side door opened, and Grandpa thrust a bundle wrapped in a heavy blanket across Miranda's lap. As Grandma pulled back the blanket, Miranda leaned forward to see what was in it. She heard a stifled whimper, and Elliot looked up at her, tears in his blue-gray eyes.

"Oh, Elliot, are you all right?" Miranda cried.

"My toes. They hurt."

Grandpa was backing the truck slowly.

"Watch for the Shady Hill's gate," he said to Grandma. "Taylor started out walking for help. He was so close to his turnoff that I'm guessing he'd walk to his house rather than heading for town, but I'm not sure."

"There it is!" said Grandma.

Miranda could barely make out the big arch over the driveway. The Shady Hills sign swayed eerily, like a pale ghost in the driving snow. Grandpa eased into the narrow road. For a way, the lane was blown clean of snow, but after rounding the first curve, a big drift loomed ahead. Grandpa stopped the truck and got out again. Soon he was back.

"It's pretty wide but not too deep. I think we can make it. There are foot tracks across it, but they're nearly blown full, so I can't tell if they're human or horse tracks."

Grandma had Elliot's shoes and socks off and was gently rubbing his feet. The tips of his toes were pure white. With his head resting on Miranda's shoulder, he squeezed Miranda's hand and choked back a body-wrenching sob.

"It's okay to cry, Elliot. I know how bad it hurts to have your feet so cold. It happened to me once."

"It hurts all the way up my legs," he whispered, "but, I don't like to be a cry baby."

"You're not a cry baby, Elliot," Miranda whispered back, kissing him on the forehead.

"How long ago did your Grandfather leave the car?" asked Grandpa.

"I don't know. It seems like a very long time," Elliot replied. "Do you think he's all right?"

"Now don't worry. We'll find him," Grandpa said.

The falling snow was thinning, and it was a little easier to see. Parts of the road were bare, while other places were covered by drifts. Elliot sat up so he could see the road. Miranda felt the tension in his firm grip on her fingers.

"There. What's that?" Miranda shouted, peering at a dark form in the road ahead.

"Yes. I see him," Grandpa said softly as he brought the truck to a stop.

Miranda watched as Grandpa pushed against the wind and bent over the dark form. She held her breath, wishing she could keep Elliot from watching. Grandpa pulled Mr. Taylor to his feet. Arms around each other, they stumbled to the truck. Miranda scooted over against Grandma to let Mr. Taylor squeeze in beside her. Grandpa helped him into the high seat. Miranda was shocked by the cold that radiated from Mr. Taylor's coat as he leaned against her. It was like pressing against a block of ice.

Grandpa revved the truck, bounced over and through drifts, and finally stopped in front of Mr. Taylor's house.

"I doubt I can make it home. After the road turns south, it'll be drifted full," Grandpa said.

"You're right. We barely made it through an hour ago," said Mr. Taylor. "You may as well stay here until the wind stops and the plow goes through."

Inside Mr. Taylor's kitchen, Grandma helped Mr. Taylor out of his frozen coat, boots, and socks and got a pan of cool water for his feet. "We'll warm it up gradually, as you can stand it," she said.

"Thank you kindly, Kathy. I bet you've done this before. This is the worst frost bite I ever got," he said. "What about the boy? Are you all right, Elliot?"

"I am now, Grandpa," Elliot answered, through chattering teeth.

Miranda wrapped a blanket around Elliot and led him to the fireplace where Grandpa had built a crackling fire. Then she went back to the kitchen to put water on for tea and hot chocolate. Turning to the window, she looked out into the storm. Snow was still whipping around, but it was thinner now. One tiny spot of blue sky appeared among the scudding gray clouds. A tear trickled down her cheek as she looked back into the living room where Grandma joked with Cash Taylor, and Grandpa cuddled Elliot in an easy chair close to the fire. Thinking how bad things could have been, she wanted to freeze this moment in time and keep these dear people beside her forever.

Chapter Seven

"Hi, pretty boy," Miranda said softly. Starlight stood in the far corner of his stall with his head down. "What's the matter? You don't look like you feel so good."

But as she approached with a palm full of oats, he raised his head and stepped toward her.

"You had me worried, boy. You must not've heard me coming, or does the cold have you down? That was quite a storm, wasn't it? Don't worry, the wind has stopped and there's a beautiful sunset. Grandma and Grandpa are waiting for me, so I've got to run, but I'll be back, I promise."

Miranda walked to the door, knowing Grandpa was anxious to get home and milk the cows. He had called to make sure the road had been cleared. Milking would be late tonight, and Miranda would have to help. She looked back one more time as she closed the stable door. Starlight usually followed and watched her leave, but today he just lay down with a groan and a deep sigh.

"You old lazy bones." Miranda called to him. "Well, get a good rest, and I'll see you tomorrow if I can."

No one would take Miranda to Shady Hills on Sunday. Her grandparents were busy digging out from the storm. Both the Langleys and the Bergmans were late getting home from trips out of town. It wasn't until after school Monday that Miranda could find a ride to Shady Hills.

"I have to beat Kimberly at the Winter Fair," Laurie said turning to look at Miranda and Chris in the back seat of her mother's car. "She told me I should withdraw before I embarrass myself."

"I wish we could've come yesterday," Miranda complained. "After school, there's hardly enough time for all of us to get a turn to ride."

"I don't have to worry about those girls. None of them ride English. My parents thought that's what I learned back east, so they're making me learn it for real," said Chris with a sigh. His lie about the classes he took at summer camp had caused him a lot of grief.

"Well, I'm riding in the trail class, and I need to work hard on that. I don't want to make any mistakes. I'll use a saddle from now on, because I'm practicing to win. I don't want to mess Queen up by falling off again," said Miranda.

"You messed yourself up pretty good when you did that," Chris reminded her.

"I rode English when I took riding lessons in Ohio. I don't know how I'll do in Western Pleasure, but it shouldn't be too hard," said Laurie.

"You look so natural on a horse, I'm sure you'll do fine." Miranda assured her friend. "Grandma said she'll find out exactly what they do in the trail class. Maybe Adam will tell you what to work on for Western Pleasure."

Miranda headed straight to Starlight's stall, while Mrs. Langley helped Chris and Laurie get Queen ready to ride. Starlight didn't get up when Miranda entered. She was alarmed. She squatted near his head and stroked his face. His eyes were dull and listless, and his nose felt warmer than usual. Clear liquid dripped from both nostrils. She couldn't see his bandaged back pastern, but the cut on his shoulder was swollen and hot.

"Oh, Starlight! You've got to drink some water. I think you have a fever again. What happened?"

She got a bucket of water from the hydrant and put it under his nose, but he refused to drink. Frantic with worry, she ran to Mr. Taylor's house and pounded on the kitchen door. There was no answer, so she turned the knob.

"Mr. Taylor!" she called, as she walked into the kitchen. "Mr. Taylor, are you home?"

She searched the house before she admitted to herself that no one was there. She ran back to the stable. Starlight's head nodded as if he were sleeping. When she called his name, he looked up, but he didn't try to stand.

"I'm going to get help for you, Starlight. I can't lose you now!"

She hurried to the tack shed and dialed Dr. Talbot's number. The veterinarian's receptionist told her that he was out on a call.

"Please have him come to Shady Hills as soon as he can. Starlight is terribly sick again," Miranda begged.

She ran back to Starlight and sat beside him on the damp wood chips that covered the floor of his stall. Looking about, she realized it hadn't been cleaned. Higgins, the old groom and sole ranch hand, usually took care of it when Miranda wasn't there. She held her beloved stallion's beautiful black head close to her body, but Starlight pulled away from her and groaned. Miranda went to find Higgins.

Running up and down the stable row, Miranda called for him. Horses nickered and stomped, but there was no sign of the old groom. Frantic and out of breath, she pounded on the door of the bunkhouse. Higgins' car was in the driveway. Why didn't he answer? She pounded again, as hard as she could. As her own breathing quieted, she heard a faint sound from within.

"Higgins?" she called. "Are you in there?"

"Come, please." The voice was barely audible.

Miranda opened the door and stepped in.

"Where are you?"

"In here. Please get me some help."

Miranda followed the feeble voice to the bedroom. Higgins was lying on the floor near the foot of the bed, under a heap of blankets.

"I wondered how long it would take before someone noticed I wasn't doing my job," he said.

"Higgins! What happened?"

"I fell getting out of bed yesterday morning. Tripped over my blankets. I must have broken something because I can't get up. Tried to crawl to the phone, but I don't have the strength to drag myself to the kitchen. I should've listened when John told me to get a phone next to the bed."

Miranda was already in the kitchen dialing 911.

"An ambulance is coming," she told the old man. "You've been lying here since yesterday morning? You must be miserable!"

"This floor's getting mighty hard, that's for sure. At least I was able to reach the blankets and cover myself up. Used one of them for a pillow." Higgins voice was weak and he seemed to be shivering.

"I'm surprised Mr. Taylor didn't come looking for you, but I don't know where he and Elliot are or how long they've been gone."

"I haven't fed or cleaned stalls for two days. The horses are probably having fits by now."

"I'll take care of them as soon as the ambulance comes," Miranda promised, "but first I gotta see what's wrong with Starlight. He won't get up."

"Call Doc Talbot."

"I did. I hope he comes soon."

"You don't need to stay here. Go see to the horses. Send the paramedics in when the ambulance comes."

"But…I don't want to leave you."

"I don't need you as much as the horses do. I'll be fine. Just get me a drink of water before you go."

Doctor Talbot hadn't arrived yet, so Miranda started her work in Starlight's stall, cleaning out all the dirty shavings and spreading fresh ones around him. She kept trying to get him to drink but he refused. Deciding there was nothing more she could do until the vet arrived, she hurried to check on the other horses. She'd filled most of the water pails when she heard sirens in the distance. Just as she watered the last horse, the ambulance crossed the cattle guard.

"This way!" she shouted, motioning for the driver to turn up the lane in front of the stable row. She ran ahead of them to the bunkhouse and opened the door for them. Before long, they carried Higgins through the living room on a metal stretcher.

"Thanks for getting me help, Miranda, and for taking care of the horses," Higgins said.

Mrs. Langley, Laurie, and Chris all crowded around Miranda as she followed the stretcher to the ambulance.

"What happened? And why on earth didn't you come get me, Miranda?" Mrs. Langley asked.

"I never thought about it after I found Higgins. I called the ambulance, and it didn't seem like there was anything else to do."

"I might have helped if you had let me know!" said Adam accusingly.

Anger blazed in his eyes, but Miranda refused to look away. She might have asked him to look at Starlight, but pride and anger rose to match his. She mirrored his scowl back at him, but he was already walking to his pickup.

Miranda called her grandma to get permission to finish the chores for Higgins and to wait for the vet. Mrs. Langley, Chris, and Laurie drove away behind Adam, leaving Miranda alone on the big ranch. She felt just a little scared, but proud, too.

There was still no sign of Doc Talbot when Miranda finished feeding. She ran back to Starlight and tried again to get him to stand. When that failed, she tried giving him sweet feed, his favorite treat, but he only turned his head away.

"Oh, Starlight, please get well. I can't lose you now. If Mr. Taylor sees you like this he might decide to put you down. You don't want to die, do you? Oh, please, Starlight, please want to live."

She called the veterinarian again and learned that he had just left the Miller ranch and was on his way to Shady Hills. Before hurrying back to Starlight's stall, Miranda got a clean towel, some antibiotic salve, and gauze. She got the towel wet at the hydrant and gently cleaned the shoulder wound. Starlight made a strange grunting sound.

"Does that make it feel better, Starlight, or worse?"

His eyes closed, and Miranda continued to stroke him with the wet towel. When she quit, he lifted his head as if to say, "Please, don't stop."

"What seems to be the trouble, here?" Miranda jumped at the rough voice.

"Mr. Taylor!" Miranda exclaimed. "I was looking for you. I don't know what happened. Starlight didn't want to get up when I got here today. I think he has fever, and his shoulder wound's all hard and swollen."

Before Mr. Taylor could answer, a truck pulled up outside. Miranda was relieved to see Doctor Talbot.

As the two men talked just outside the door, Miranda strained to listen, full of fear that Mr. Taylor would tell the vet not to bother. This would just cost him more money.

"Doesn't look good." It was Cash Taylor's voice.

"One shot might do it, if it's big enough," she heard the vet say. *What! A lethal injection?* She gasped at the thought and huddled closer to Starlight.

Doc Talbot pushed into the stall and knelt beside Miranda and Starlight.

"The shoulder wound is hard as a rock. I'm going to have to open it up and let it drain." Doctor Talbot seemed to be talking to no one in particular, but his voice was calm and soothing. "How does his back pastern look?"

"I don't know. I haven't been able to get him up so I can see it."

"Well, let me lance his shoulder before we try to move him. I don't think you want to watch this."

"Oh, but I do!" Miranda exclaimed.

Mr. Taylor was back with a scowl on his face.

"I just checked the other horses. Not one of them, except Queen, has a clean stall. Where's Higgins?"

"Oh, I forgot to tell you. He went to the hospital in the ambulance."

"What? How could you forget a thing like that? What happened?"

Miranda told Mr. Taylor all about it and added, "I fed and watered, but there wasn't time to clean stalls."

"Well, it's got to be done. We'll have more sick horses if we don't keep them clean and dry. Would you help me while Doc takes care of Starlight?"

They're trying to get me out of the way so that they can put Starlight to sleep — forever, Miranda thought.

Chapter Eight

Miranda argued. She begged. "I need to stay with Starlight. He trusts me. Please don't do anything to hurt him. He's come a long way. He can get over this."

"The doctor can take care of Starlight without your help," Mr. Taylor said, taking her by the arm and pulling her from the stall. "No one should have to watch this. Besides, I need your help so I can get done and go get Elliot."

"Where is Elliot?"

"He went to Mark's house after school. I had to take a couple of horses to Billings today. Had a buyer over there, if I'd deliver. I should probably go get Elliot now, but these stalls have to be cleaned."

"I'll clean them while you go get him," Miranda said.

"No, just help me, and then I'll take you home," Mr Taylor said, leaving no room for argument. "I'll get Elliot on the way to your house."

When the last stall was finally done, she dashed to Starlight's stall. Seeing him lying on his side, his head flat against the floor, Miranda gasped. But Doctor Talbot knelt at his side, smoothing a wet plaster cast that covered his hoof and extended to just above the fetlock.

"What have you done to him?" Miranda asked.

"I'm immobilizing his leg so he doesn't keep breaking the wound open. If we can just get rid of the infection, he should recover nicely. I've given him a double dose of penicillin. We'll keep him on antibiotics for a couple of weeks and I think he'll be just fine." Looking at Miranda's stricken face, he added, "He's just resting. I gave him a light sedative so I could work on his foot. He'll be up and around soon."

Miranda sat down beside Starlight's head and stroked his face. His eyes fluttered and slowly opened.

Mr. Taylor took the back road to her house so he could stop at the Wagner ranch to get Elliot. As they pulled into the driveway of the large house, Mr. Taylor honked.

Elliot ran out. "Oh, Grandfather," Elliot said as he slid into the back seat, "I had such a good time. We rode horses all afternoon, and I'm very good at it. May I ride your horses now?"

"I've told you time and again that you could ride after you have lessons, not before!" Mr. Taylor shouted. "I can't believe you rode when I told you not to!"

Miranda saw the happiness vanish from Elliot's face.

"But, Grandfather," Elliot began, "Mark and his brother taught me, isn't that the same as lessons?"

"No, it's not. Don't you get on anyone's horse until I say you can!"

Miranda flinched. She cast Elliot a look of sympathy, but he was looking down and didn't see.

"Bye, Elliot. I'll see you tomorrow." She slammed the door without a word of thanks to Mr. Taylor.

"Is your grumpy grandpa still being a grouch?" Miranda asked Elliot Tuesday morning when she met him in the hallway at school.

"I guess he was worried about me, Miranda. And about Higgins, too," Elliot said.

"That's no excuse for biting your head off," Miranda said. "How is Higgins; have you heard?"

"His hip is broken. He has to have surgery today, so Grandfather went to Bozeman. He wants to be there when Higgins gets out of the operating room."

Miranda found it hard to concentrate on her school work. She was still mad at Mr. Taylor for his angry words to Elliot. Worry about Higgins going into surgery swirled through her head, too, all mixed up with the anger. People died in surgery sometimes. Miranda shook her head to get rid of such thoughts. She couldn't imagine Shady Hills without Higgins. When the last bell finally rang, Miranda hurried to the office to call her grandmother.

"Laurie's Mom can't go to Shady Hills today. Can you take us?"

"No, I'm sorry, Miranda. I have to help Grandpa vaccinate some calves before chore time."

"Then may I ride Elliot's bus?" Miranda begged. "Higgins is in the hospital. I can help with his chores."

"Okay, but call me as soon as you're done."

Mr. Taylor was waiting for them at the gate.

"What are you doing here?" he asked bluntly as Miranda climbed into his car.

"I came to do Higgins' chores for him. I'll come do them every day until he gets well. He is going to get well, isn't he?"

"He came through surgery okay, but who knows when he'll be able to work. Do you think all his work was done in a few hours in the afternoon? Higgins has been my right hand man for thirty years. It won't be easy to replace him. He didn't just feed horses and clean stalls. He trained my colts and kept an eye on every animal I own. He knew exactly when a mare was in season, he knew each foal's habits and personality. He told me which ones should be groomed for the track, which ones would make good brood mares and sires. No, I couldn't replace Higgins with a dozen men, let alone a scrawny little girl."

"I know I can't do everything he did, but I can do everything I can, and that might be better than nothing," Miranda said, blinking back tears. "Oh, why did he have to break his hip?"

"Higgins is seventy-five years old. He's worked hard all his life. I tried to get more help so he wouldn't have to do so much. No one ever lasted," Mr. Taylor said more softly. His deep voice cracked as if he were about to cry, too.

Miranda went to Shady Hills every day after school and helped with the afternoon chores before taking her turn on Queen. Mr. Taylor didn't look much younger than Higgins, so this work was probably hard on him, too. Yet, as long as he didn't find a new hired man, Miranda held on to the hope that Higgins would be back.

Rushing into Starlight's stall one cold afternoon in mid December, Miranda bumped into a tall, thin man in a dark wool coat.

"Oh," she cried. "What are you doing to Starlight?"

"I'm trying to do my job. What are you doing, barging in here?"

Starlight was hunched in the corner of his stall, every muscle tense, eyes wide, and nostrils flared. The man held a pitchfork in front of him like a weapon, the sharp tines aimed at Starlight.

"Get on out of this stall," the man ordered. "This horse is dangerous. He ought to be shot."

"YOU get out! You're scaring Starlight! I'll take care of him. You have no reason to be in my horse's stall!" Miranda stood defiantly between the horse and the man.

"That horse is a demon! He attacked me."

"Get out and don't ever touch Starlight again!" She reached for the pitchfork.

The man grabbed Miranda by the arm, hurled her out the door, and slammed it shut.

"You have the wrong horse. This is Jet Propelled Cadillac, and he's a maniac. I'm going to show him who's boss," the man sneered as he closed the top half of the dutch door and latched it from the inside.

Rushing through the next stall, Miranda climbed onto

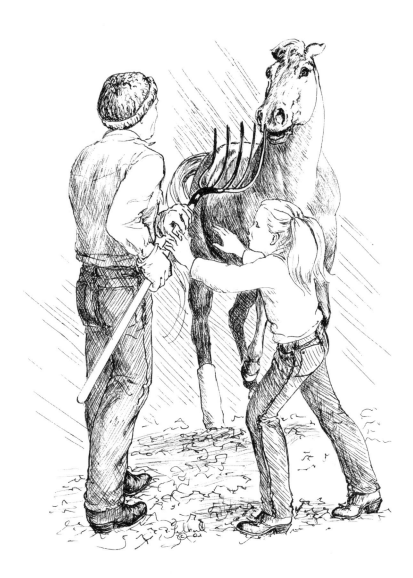

the fence dividing the paddocks, hoping that the back door to Starlight's stall would be open. The lower half of the dutch door was latched from the inside, but the top was slightly ajar. Miranda pulled it open with her toe, and from the fence, stepped on the lower half and jumped inside.

In the dimly lit stall, she could only see the man's outline. He was holding the pitchfork like a bat, ready to swing.

"Stop it!" Miranda lunged for the pitchfork.

The man staggered, almost fell, then regained his balance. With a murderous squeal, Starlight bared his teeth and clamped down on the man's upper arm. Shaking his head, Starlight dragged the man off his feet. Miranda opened the front stall door, and the man stumbled out. She closed the door and latched it.

"You're crazy! That horse is a killer," the man shouted. "He'll have to go if I'm going to work here."

Starlight had backed into the corner again, neck arched, eyes wide, snorting loudly.

"Starlight, what did he do to you? I'm so sorry. I'll make sure he doesn't get near you ever again!" Miranda exclaimed. In a soothing tone, she added. "I wish Higgins were here. If that monster is supposed to take his place, Mr. Taylor has made a big mistake. I'll tell him so, too. When he finds out what that guy was doing, he'll kick him off this place and tell him never to come back."

As she stroked Starlight's neck and his face, he began to calm down. He finally pressed his face against her.

Miranda fed and watered him. She was examining his shoulder wound when a booming voice made her jump.

"What's going on in here, Miranda?" Mr. Taylor asked, scowling at her over the lower door.

"I'm taking care of Starlight! A big, ugly man poked him with a pitchfork…that man right there," she added as the man's grizzled face loomed behind Mr. Taylor.

"I heard all about it," Mr. Taylor said. "He says when he stepped in to clean, Starlight, I mean Sir Jet, attacked him. Hicks said he tried to protect you, and the horse actually bit him! I think you'd better stay out of this stall until we find out what's gotten into him."

"What's gotten into him?" Miranda repeated, dumfounded. "This man was attacking him with a pitchfork. Nothing's wrong with Starlight. He's as gentle with me as ever. He was just trying to defend himself. You can see that, can't you?"

Miranda leaned against Starlight and patted his neck to prove it, but Starlight tensed and snorted as the tall man leaned over the door beside Mr. Taylor.

"See what I'm tellin' ya, boss?" the man said.

"Come out, Miranda," Mr. Taylor commanded in a voice that left no room for argument. He held the door for her.

She obeyed, and Mr. Taylor closed both the bottom and the top halves of the door.

"Mr. Taylor, I swear, Starlight would never hurt me. This man did something to him. You shouldn't let him near your horses. You know Higgins would never treat a horse like that."

"Miranda, did you see the man hit Sir Jet with the pitchfork?"

"I saw him getting ready to. I don't know what he did before I got here. Starlight was scared to death, all hunched up in the corner."

"You didn't see this man do anything to provoke Sir Jet," Mr. Taylor said, "and he says he didn't."

"That's right," growled the man.

"That's a lie!" Miranda shouted.

With a look of pure hatred, the man stepped toward her with clenched fists. Mr. Taylor didn't seem to notice.

"Miranda, I don't like it, but I can't take a chance on you getting hurt by a horse that's gone loco. It happens sometimes, and Sir Jet has been through a lot," Mr. Taylor said solemnly. "This is Martin Hicks. I hired him to feed, clean stalls, and do some of the maintenance around here. I'm still looking for a new trainer."

"Please don't let him take care of your horses! Please, Mr. Taylor. He doesn't treat horses like you and Higgins do. He'll beat them."

"That's enough! I don't need you telling me how to run my ranch. You stick to helping Chris with Queen. Stay away from the other horses unless I ask for your help."

Tears sprang into Miranda's eyes, and she sputtered angrily before turning and running toward the arena. She sat on the platform and cried silently as she feigned watching Laurie put Queen through her paces.

Chris saw her and asked, "What's wrong with you?"

"None of your business!" Miranda snapped.

"Chill out, Miranda," Chris said. "I'm just asking."

Chris really did seem to care, but she couldn't talk about it without crying.

"I'll tell you later," she said.

Adam left, and it was Miranda's turn to ride Queen. Her heart wasn't in it, and she quit before her time was up. After helping to put the tack away, she slipped into Queen's stall, and brushed the mare's satin coat as her mind raced. She heard voices.

"If you want me to stay around, you're going to have to get rid of that black devil. He's a killer. I'm not going to put my life in danger again to clean his stall."

"Don't worry," she heard Mr. Taylor answer gruffly. "I'll see that you don't have to go near him."

At the dinner table that evening, Miranda told her grandparents everything that had happened that day. She described Starlight's fear, the man's rage, and repeated every word she had heard Hicks and Mr. Taylor say.

"You've got to help me save Starlight," she begged. "Mr. Taylor won't listen to me, and he's going to get rid of him after all we've done to save him—just because of that horrible man."

"I don't know what we can do," Grandpa said. "The horse belongs to Mr. Taylor, and he knows horses. If he thinks Starlight's dangerous, well, maybe he is."

"Miranda, horses do go loco. I don't want you putting yourself in danger for that horse," Grandma added. "I know you love him, but for your own sake, stay away from him."

Chapter Nine

Miranda lay awake, waiting for her grandparents to turn out the lights and go to bed. Even then she could hear the drone of their voices from their bedroom across the hall. She wondered if they would ever go to sleep. Miranda's eyes grew heavy and she dreamed she was riding Starlight. She leaned into his mane and whispered, "Faster, faster," until Starlight was soaring over a dark chasm. And then they fell, the black horse beneath her flailing in the air. Miranda's body jerked, and she awakened. Shakily, she tiptoed into the kitchen and looked at the clock on the microwave: 12:35. Opening the door to the storage room, she reached for her backpack where it hung, with her sleeping bag already tied to it, next to the larger ones that belonged to her grandparents.

Miranda tiptoed to her bedroom and filled it with a change of clothes, extra socks, her flashlight and a book. She put on a wool hat, mittens, her snow-boots, and her warmest coat. In the kitchen, she added as much food as her backpack would hold—cheese, bread, crackers and raisins. She filled her pockets with apples and carrots and stuffed some newspaper and a box of kitchen matches into the map pocket of her backpack. The hinges squeaked when she opened the back door and, holding her breath, stole out into the cold.

Miranda shouldered into the heavy pack and trudged into the night. When head lights appeared behind her, she dropped and lay flat in the ditch until the car zoomed past. From the school, she cut across the field and hurried to Shady Hills, working up a sweat beneath her heavy clothes. Gasping for breath, she opened the top half of Starlight's door and peered in. It was pitch dark inside, and she could hear nothing but her own breathing. She fumbled for the flashlight in the side pocket of her backpack, closed her eyes, and switched it on. Uttering a desperate prayer, she opened her eyes and saw Starlight staring into the light from where he lay in the corner of his stall.

"Oh, Starlight, thank heaven you're still alive."

She hurried into his stall, closed the door, and latched it. Starlight scrambled to his feet, rumbled a greeting, and thrust his nose against her pocket where she often carried treats for him. Laughing, she fed him a carrot.

"I've got to get some grain. Then we're going for a walk, Starlight."

The going was slow, not so much because of Starlight's limp, as the heavy burden Miranda carried. She was so tired she could hardly put one foot in front of the other. When she left the bridle path and started uphill into a wooded area, she sat down and shrugged out of her backpack.

"I'm going to leave this and the grain here. I'll come back for them after I get you to the cave."

With only the narrow beam of her flashlight to guide her, Miranda wasn't sure where she was. She wandered for what seemed hours, Starlight right behind her. She could feel his excitement. He snorted occasionally, blowing a large puff of steamy breath into the back of her neck. He almost stepped on her a couple of times; at other times he stopped so abruptly that the lead rope tightened and almost pulled her over backward. Finally, in the sweeping beam of her flashlight, she saw a rocky cliff to her right. She headed toward it, shining her light on it every few seconds to keep her bearing. Starlight stumbled a couple of times as they zig-zagged up the hill, but at last they stood in front of the cave opening.

Starlight shied nervously.

"It's all right, boy," Miranda said softly.

She petted him and offered another carrot. He snorted, shuddered, but took the carrot from her hand. After coaxing him farther into the entrance with three more carrots, she found a protruding rock and tied him to it.

"You stay here. I'll be back in a little while with your grain and my pack. Here's another carrot. Just wait here."

With the aid of her flashlight, Miranda followed her tracks back down the hill. It began to snow lightly. Going down the hill didn't take long, but climbing back up was hard work. Half way up the steepest part, she decided to leave the back pack and take only the grain. She could feed some to Starlight, make sure he was okay, and then run back for the rest of her load. But, when she finally stumbled into the cave, it was empty.

Dropping the heavy feed sack, she rushed in, calling his name. He was gone—lead rope and all. Frantic with fear, she called his name as she searched, making larger and larger circles, finally retracing her steps toward Shady Hills. It was snowing harder now. The flurry of downy flakes made it hard to see. Fearing Starlight had gone back to where his life was in danger, she began to cry. By the time she reached her backpack, she dropped to the ground, sobbing, more tired and discouraged than she'd ever been before.

She didn't know how long she lay there crying before

feeling warm breath on the back of her neck. She turned over and sat up. Starlight sniffed her and nudged her with his nose. "Oh, Starlight," she cried, jumping up and hugging him. "You scared me so bad! I was afraid I'd never see you again."

Slipping into her backpack and looping the lead rope over her shoulder, Miranda started back up the hill. Starlight followed like a puppy, pausing to rest whenever she did. A pile of sweet feed in the back of the big room was all the coaxing it took to get Starlight inside. Miranda gathered wood and built a small fire at the cave's entrance. Exploring passages leading from the main chamber, she found the room she'd seen on her first visit. It was farther out of the wind, out of sight, and had room enough for both her and Starlight to lie down.

Too tired to be hungry, Miranda slowly realized she was thirsty. Water! She'd forgotten to bring anything to drink. Her thirst grew to an acute craving. They were far above the river, and she had no bucket for carrying water. Starlight could survive on snow, at least for awhile, but could she? Searching in her backpack, she found a metal cup and went outside to pack it full of snow. She ate a few mouthfuls, as well. It did little to slake her thirst.

Setting the cup near the fire, Miranda went to check on Starlight. He'd finished his grain, so she tried coaxing him into the smaller room. The passageway was narrow, and he wanted no part of it. She coaxed, bribed, tugged and pushed, but to no avail.

Frustrated, she said, "All right, have it your way, but you'd be warmer back there."

She tied him to a large log that she managed to drag in from the entrance. She knew it wouldn't stop him if he wanted to go, but maybe it would slow him down. She checked her cup. The snow had melted leaving less than an inch of water. After gulping it down, she packed and heaped her cup with snow again and set it by the fire. In the smaller room, she spread out her sleeping bag and pulled off her coat. Folding it for a pillow, she crawled into the cold bag, wondering if the snow in her cup had melted yet.

Shivering, she lay wide awake, listening. A scraping noise echoed from the other room. She got up to find Starlight was dragging the log, not to go out, but toward her. Untying his lead rope, she led him to the dying fire. She drank the few swallows of water from her cup and, leading Starlight, returned to her sleeping bag and crawled in. Starlight seemed to want her company as much as she did his. He lay beside her on the sandy floor. Turning off the light, she smiled in the darkness.

Miranda awakened to total darkness, blinked her eyes, and wondered if the electricity had gone off. The house was never this dark. She turned onto her back and stretched before remembering she was sleeping in a cave. She groped for her flashlight tucked under the coat beneath her head. Switching it on, she shined it on the empty ground where Starlight had lain beside her.

She wiggled out of her sleeping bag and hurried toward the entrance. Starlight stood in the large opening, darkly silhouetted against dazzling, white snow. She spoke his name and walked to his side. He rumbled a greeting and then lowered his head to mouth some of the fluffy snow that had fallen during the night. The sun was almost directly overhead. She squinted in the light reflected from the snow—a nice thick blanket that covered all their tracks. She was glad for that, but it would make finding grass for Starlight harder.

Miranda poured sweet feed on the floor for Starlight and dug out bread and cheese for herself. She looked out over the white-robed treetops down to the mostly frozen river that wound through the pasture below. It was easy to imagine they were alone in the world. Not a house, car, or any other sign of civilization could be seen or heard.

After eating, Miranda waded into the snow in search of firewood and grass she could pick for Starlight to eat. Pulling back some branches of a fallen tree, she found long thick grass, brown from the winter cold, but still good feed. She was bending over to pull some when a shove from behind landed her head first in snow covered branches.

"Hey!" she shouted, struggling to her feet.

Starlight shook his head playfully and pawed the snow. He stretched his long neck and began nibbling dry grass from under the branch.

"Starlight," Miranda laughed, "I thought you were still back in the cave. You almost gave me a heart attack."

Starlight saved her the trouble of picking grass for him. As he grazed, she dragged deadwood to the cave and piled it just inside. The exertion soon had her sweating in spite of the freezing temperature. By the time Starlight came hobbling back, she had piled up enough wood to last two or three days.

She watched her horse proudly—well, she thought of him as her own. He limped of course, because of the plaster cast on his ankle, but he seemed strong and vigorous. She no longer worried that he would wander back to the stable. He seemed happy to be here with her. He was in his element now. His free spirit was never meant to be locked up in a twelve- by twelve-foot stall. Proving he could take care of himself, he ate snow for his water and foraged for food. Yes, Miranda decided, they were both born for this life. If only they could live forever without the confines of walls or fences; without people telling them what to do.

Darkness came quickly and Miranda struggled to build a fire before the dim light coming in the cave faded away completely. The wood was wet and refused to burn. She used up most of her newspaper and was about to give up, afraid she'd run out of matches, too, when a glowing spark burst into flame. She fanned it to life and it smoldered for a few minutes. Carefully adding more twigs she blew on it to keep it going. At last it was blazing on its own. She went outside and filled her cup with snow.

When Miranda came back, the flame was out and dark smoke billowed in its place. She fanned it to life again. It was a struggle to keep it going with small twigs. She finally thought it was safe to add a large branch, but when she put it on, the flame died, releasing a plume of dark smoke. She didn't have the energy to try again, so she followed Starlight's example and ate snow, letting it dissolve slowly in her mouth. It didn't quench her thirst, but it helped. After dining on more bread and cheese, she shared an apple with Starlight.

After her meager supper, she could think of nothing to do. The moon wasn't up yet, and she couldn't see beyond the cave door. For the first time since leaving the house, she began to question her plan. What about Grandma and Grandpa? Would they be worried sick or just very angry? Would their feelings be hurt that she had run away? What if they didn't find the note she'd left? Even if they did, would they understand? She hadn't wanted to give away her hide-out, but she hated to have them worry. She had written:

> Please don't worry and don't be mad. If you really know me, you must understand that I can't just let him die. I will be safe, so don't call the cops.
> Love, Miranda.

She hoped it was enough to make them understand that she wasn't doing this to hurt them. They had always told her she could come to them for help when she was in trouble, but when she did, they had let her down. Having only herself to depend on, she did what she had to do. Over and over she told herself these things, but it didn't make her feel better.

The cave was dark and cold. She longed for the warmth and brightness of her grandmother's kitchen. An owl hooted somewhere in the distance, another answered from so close that she jumped. She sat motionless, her body tense and shaking, but when the howls of a pack of coyotes rose to a string of high pitched yips, she crept to the back room of the cave.

Her flashlight was growing dim as she changed into dry clothes before crawling into her sleeping bag. Why hadn't she brought extra batteries? The light slowly faded to nothing, and panic took the place of the peace that had warmed her during the day. She shivered as she felt her way into her sleeping bag.

"I'm in here, Starlight. Please come here and sleep with me again."

Ashamed of her fright and her tears, she was glad no one was there to witness them. She heard Starlight dragging his lame foot across the cave floor. She turned the flashlight back on and shook it. It glowed faintly, long enough for her to see him coming. He lay down beside her. She scooted close, pressing against his warm body.

Chapter Ten

A blinding light forced Miranda's eyes to close all the more tightly as it awakened her. She put her hands to her face and turned her head.

Voices echoed eerily, bouncing off walls, frightening her. She sat up, half asleep and confused.

"Miranda, are you all right?" It was Grandma's voice, full of concern.

"You crazy kid! I can't believe you'd come out here in the middle of winter all by yourself," said Mr. Taylor. He sounded more amazed than angry.

"You all right, Mandy?" asked Grandpa.

"Yes! I'm fine. Where's Starlight?" Miranda's voice rose in sudden fear and she struggled to her feet. "You didn't take him out and shoot him, did you?"

"He's right here, Miranda," called Elliot. "I'm giving him more of the grain from this sack. I hope you don't mind."

"Did you really think I was going to kill him?" asked Mr. Taylor as they all gathered around Starlight near the mouth of the cave. "Is that why you stole him away in the middle of the night?"

"Well, yes! I heard you tell that terrible hired man that you would see to it. He told you to get rid of him, and you said you would!" Miranda said, hotly. "I'm sorry about taking your property again, but you know I can't let you kill him. Please don't, I'd rather die myself."

"I never had any intention of taking orders from Martin Hicks!" Cash Taylor exclaimed. "I said I'd see that he didn't have to worry about this horse, but not because I was about to get rid of any of my horses on his recommendation. After what you said, I watched him around the horses, and he upset them all. No, the reason I said he didn't have to worry is because he wasn't going to be working for me anymore. I sent him hiking."

"Oh!" Miranda grinned, and her face grew hot.

"When I went out the next morning and found Sir Jet gone," Mr. Taylor continued, "I thought Hicks had done something to him to get revenge for being fired. He's just the kind of person who'd do such a thing. But when your grandparents came along with that note from you, I knew you and Starlight were together."

"How did you find us?" Miranda asked, happy to hear Mr. Taylor use her name for the black colt.

"Well now, that wasn't too hard, but I would've found you a whole lot quicker if I'd known this cave was here. It's hard to believe I never stumbled onto it before, but you gotta admit it's pretty well hidden."

"None of us had any idea where you would go for shelter. We called Chris and Laurie, thinking they might be in on it, but they didn't know anything," Grandma explained. "We drove all over the neighborhood, even looked into that old shed by the school. The snow covered your tracks completely."

"It was Elliot who thought you might have hidden in the woods somewhere, so we saddled up three of my horses and started searching the river pasture," Mr. Taylor added. "We had given up and headed back to the stables when your grandma smelled smoke. It was too dark to see anything,

even with the full moon, but we let Kathy's sharp nose lead us up the hill to where the snow's all trampled down. Then it was an easy matter to follow your tracks to the cave."

"That's where Starlight was eating. There's good grass under the snow."

"Shall we head back?" Grandpa asked. "I tied your bedroll to your pack and strapped it behind my saddle."

"I'm riding with Grandfather," Elliot said with a sigh. "If I had my own horse you could ride with me."

Miranda rode behind her grandmother, holding Starlight's lead rope. She looked back to make sure they weren't going too fast for him. He followed closely as he looked around him, ears pricked forward and neck arched. Mr. Taylor, with Elliot in front of him on his big gelding, Commander, rode behind Starlight.

"And how come you got to stay up and ride in the middle of the night?" Miranda called back to him.

"It's not the middle of the night," Elliot said, pushing the button on his glow-light watch. "It's only nine o'clock."

Christmas was fast approaching. As Miranda soaked in the bathtub, she wondered how she'd buy anyone gifts. She had no money. In just a few hours, she had to sing with the rest of the fifth and sixth graders in front of an audience. The annual school program featured a silly play by the lower grades about a reindeer who had no gift for Santa. Miranda didn't want to go. She was sick of the play and the songs they'd been rehearsing. A call from her mother had put her in a bad mood.

"I'm sorry I haven't mailed you anything yet," Mom said. "I just haven't had time to go shopping." But then she went on to talk about a cute mechanical dog she bought for Kort, the little kid she took care of. "I just can't wait to see him open it," Mom had said.

When the program was finally over, Miranda waited in the auditorium for her grandparents to quit talking to the neighbors they hadn't seen all winter. She just wanted to go home.

"Have you seen Elliot?" asked a familiar voice.

"Oh, hi, Mr. Taylor. No, I haven't, but wasn't he cute in his little elf costume?"

"Yes, but these programs tire me to death. Would you help me find him, so I can go home?"

Miranda wandered down the hall looking at all the excited little kids exclaiming over their bags from Santa. She peeked in Elliot's classroom, didn't see anyone, and was about to leave when she heard voices.

"I don't think he's even thought about a Christmas present for me. If he asked me what I wanted I'd tell him riding lessons," Elliot said.

"If you need more lessons, I'll teach you. You rode just fine at my house the other day. If your grandpa wants a grown up to teach you, my brother or my dad could," Mark answered.

"He says he wants to teach me himself or hire an English riding instructor. He says he doesn't want me to get hurt, and he wants me to learn properly, so I won't have bad habits to break."

"Doesn't he think we ride properly?" Mark asked. "I bet I can ride better than he can."

"Elliot, your grandfather is looking for you," Miranda interrupted. Mr. Taylor was behind her, and she hoped he hadn't heard Elliot's conversation—or maybe it would be a good thing if he did.

After school the next Monday, Miranda boarded Elliot's bus, since neither Chris nor Laurie were going to Shady Hills. She asked Elliot if she could sit beside him. He grinned and scooted closer to Mark to make room for her.

When the bus stopped at the gate to the Shady Hills Ranch, there was no Cadillac waiting for them.

"Well, looks like we have to walk. Are you warm enough?" Miranda asked, eyeing Elliot's bare head.

"I have a cap in my backpack," he answered. "Besides, walking will keep us warm."

"I guess it will. At least the wind isn't blowing, or if it is, these trees are stopping it."

"The wind never blows here, but wait until we get out in the open."

"What do you want for Christmas, Elliot?" Miranda asked as they walked.

"Oh, nothing much," Elliot said with a sigh. "You don't need to get me anything, Miranda."

"Well," Miranda stammered, "I'd like to get you something, but what I meant was, what are you going to ask your Grandfather to give you."

"Oh, I can't ask for anything. That's rude!"

"But it's Christmas. Everyone asks for something at Christmas time."

"Not everyone. I don't. Neither did Mum."

"Why not?"

"Mum said Christmas should be about giving, not getting. So we always looked for people who had less than we did. We spent our Christmas money on them."

"Really?" Miranda asked. "You didn't get anything?"

"I always got what I needed whenever I needed it."

"What did you do on Christmas day, if you had no presents?"

"Oh, I usually had something, and I always gave Mum something. But the best part was giving. Then we'd have a big meal and invite some family who didn't have a place to go. It was fun, and I made new friends."

"Wow, how unusual. It sounds pretty cool, though."

"Uh huh, it was. I really miss Mum at Christmas time," Elliot sighed. "I should be thinking what to give Grandfather, not about what he can give me."

"Well, I don't think it's wrong to wish for what you want. I believe if you wish long enough and hard enough, you'll get what you wish for." Miranda was sure Elliot wanted a horse just as much as she did. His grandfather had so many, it just seemed wrong that Mr. Taylor wouldn't let him ride.

"I wonder what has become of Grandfather," Elliot said, interrupting her reverie. "He has never been so late before. One time I was halfway home before he came up behind me. He said he was sorry for being late, and I told him it was okay. After all, I'm not a baby."

"Maybe he went to Bozeman to see Higgins."

"Yes, he may have. I'm sure he'll be along soon, and even if he isn't, it's okay. You're here."

But they made it all the way to the stables on foot. Elliot looked in the garage.

"The car is gone. Grandfather isn't home."

"Do you want to come with me to clean stalls and check on the horses' feed and water?"

Elliot tagged along cheerfully as Miranda started down the stable row. The first stall was immaculate, the water trough brim full, and the buckskin mare was lazily munching hay. Peering over the lower half of the stall door, she studied the horse carefully.

"Hey, I remember this horse. I haven't seen her in the stable before, though," Miranda said.

"Then where have you seen it?" asked Elliot.

"This is the mare I rode the first time I saw your grandfather," Miranda explained. "Boy, was he ever mad."

"What happened?"

"I was at school, and Chris dared me to ride the horses in the field. They were just across the fence—Starlight and this mare. I tried to get on Starlight, but he was wild then, so I got on this one. She was gentle as could be, until Starlight started chasing her. He ran her all the way back to the barn. Mr. Taylor was waiting for me."

"What did he do?"

"Just yelled at me," Miranda answered, making it sound as if it was nothing, but she'd never forget how frightened she had been at the time. He had told her to stay off his ranch, a command she had not obeyed.

"Weren't you afraid of falling off when Starlight was chasing you?"

"Nah! This mare is easy to ride," Miranda said, an idea brewing in her mind. "Want to pet her? Let's go in so you can see her better. You'll see what a sweetheart she is."

Elliot promptly stepped up to the mare's side and began patting her shoulder.

"She is a very nice horse," he said.

Miranda lifted Elliot.

"Grab her mane and pull yourself up," she said, pushing him.

Elliot straddled the mare, a big smile on his face as he patted her withers.

I will make his wish come true, Miranda thought. "Should I go get a halter and lead her around for you?"

Suddenly Elliot's smile disappeared, and Miranda heard a car rattle across the cattle guard.

"Help me down," Elliot begged. "I'm not supposed to be riding."

Chapter Eleven

So much for making wishes come true, Miranda thought as she headed for Starlight's stall. Elliot hadn't looked at all happy when he slid off the buckskin's back, hurried out the door, and ran to the house. Miranda almost ran into Adam Barber coming out with a fork full of dirty shavings.

"What are you doing here?" she asked, jumping out of the way of the pitchfork.

"I'm Mr. Taylor's new groom, trainer, and manure shoveler," he said with a grin. "If I'd known you were coming, I would've saved this stall for you to clean."

Miranda's jaw dropped as Adam turned and pushed the wheelbarrow to the next stall, whistling a happy tune.

Christmas day dawned bright and clear on freshly fallen snow. Miranda hurried outside to feed the chickens and her bunnies as she did every morning.

"Merry Christmas, chickens! And Merry Christmas, to you Barkley, you beautiful rooster," she sang as she filled their feeders. Miranda filled the waterer, which consisted of a small circular trough screwed onto a Mason jar. When turned upside down, the water from the jar kept the little trough brim full but would never overflow. Then she turned to her rabbits. "Merry Christmas, Patches. Here is a carrot and a lettuce leaf for you. And one for you, Mopsy," she said as she petted each one in their separate hutches after giving them more alfalfa pellets and fresh water.

When she finished, she offered to help Grandpa clean the barn. He said he was almost done, so she could go help Grandma, who was bucket-feeding the calves in the shed. It was a job Miranda loved.

"I've fed all but those three," Grandma said. "If you want to finish, I'll go cook breakfast."

When the chores were done, they all sat down to a breakfast of ham and eggs and biscuits with gravy.

"I bet Laurie and Chris have already opened their presents," Miranda said, eyeing the sparkling Christmas tree and the brightly wrapped gifts piled beneath it.

"We've done half a day's work already, and I'm starved," Grandpa laughed. "Enjoy your breakfast; the gifts aren't going anywhere."

Miranda got a pair of socks from her great-grandmother Morrison who lived in Colorado, and a pair of jeans from her aunt and uncle. Grandma gave her a western style shirt, a book about horses, and a watch. The last gift she opened was from Grandpa. She gasped as she pulled the lid off a box of dark brown cowboy boots. She tried them on immediately, and they fit perfectly.

"Oh, Grandpa, thank you!" Miranda cried. "Thank you, too, Grandma. Now I have everything I need to ride in the horse show. I must call Uncle Corey and Aunt Jolene to thank them for the Levis."

Grandma and Grandpa were both pleased with the simple cards she had made for them. Tears came to Grandma's eyes when she read hers, and Grandpa smiled and hugged her after looking at his. Miranda wished she could have given them more, but they seemed happy with the simple colored drawings and the message of her love and appreciation.

After the living room was cleaned up and the breakfast dishes done, Miranda asked if she could make two cakes. "One for Mr. Taylor and Elliot, and one for Starlight."

Grandma helped her make a carrot cake that went light on the sugar and heavy on the carrots. They made a beautiful chocolate layer cake as well.

Mr. Taylor welcomed them warmly, invited them in, and offered them hot cider. He and Elliot had been playing chess, but they abandoned their game and gathered around the kitchen table.

"I'll be right back. I have something for Starlight," Miranda said. "Do you want to go with me, Elliot?"

Elliot put on his coat, slipped into his boots, and followed Miranda. Starlight nickered when he saw them.

"Merry Christmas to you, too, Starlight!" Miranda shouted with a laugh. She gave him the cake, breaking off small pieces and putting them in his mouth. He ate greedily and nudged her hand for more. Elliot fed him some of the cake, giggling as Starlight's velvety lips tickled his palm. Miranda saw that his stall and his bandages were clean, and he had plenty of water and hay.

"I helped Grandfather and Adam. We got all the chores done just before you got here," Elliot explained.

"Is the buckskin mare still in her stall?" Miranda asked.

"Yes," Elliot said, "and I found out what her name is and why Grandfather brought her in. Since she isn't going to have a foal this spring, he wants to sell her. He's keeping her in so people can look at her."

"Sell her? That's terrible! Just because she isn't going to make him money this spring. Why does your Grandfather only think of money?" Miranda asked.

"He doesn't, Miranda. If he did, he wouldn't have me."

"No, I guess he wouldn't. Sorry, Elliot. I shouldn't get so mad. I know your grandfather is a good man—deep down."

"Can we give Lady some of this cake?" Elliot asked.

"Lady? Is that the buckskin's name?" Miranda asked.

"Grand Cadillac's Ladyslipper," Elliot replied,"Lady for short. I like that name. It fits her."

"Yes, she's a lady, all right," Miranda agreed. "There's a little cake left. Let's feed it to her. Goodbye, Starlight."

After feeding Lady, Miranda asked Elliot if he wanted to sit on her again.

"I'm not supposed to, Miranda."

"It's not actually riding. What can it hurt? It'll be my Christmas present to you."

Elliot nodded and let Miranda boost him on.

"I don't think I should be doing this, but I love horses so much, it's hard to watch other people riding all the time when I can't. I look at all these horses everyday and help take care of them sometimes, but Grandfather is afraid I might get hurt."

"Maybe, but I don't really understand why. I bet he rode when he was your age." *If he wants to teach him, he should be doing it.* Changing the subject she asked, "Did he get you anything for Christmas?"

"A toy truck and a hand held video baseball game."

"I would think he could see that riding lessons would have been a better present," Miranda said, sensing his disappointment.

Elliot shrugged.

Miranda wished she could make Mr. Taylor understand and care about his grandson's feelings. A baseball game! Elliot had never played baseball in his life and had no interest in it. What was the old man thinking?

"Let's go play in the snow for a bit," Elliot suggested, sliding off the mare and landing on his seat.

Miranda's anger melted as they tossed fluffy snow at each other. A half hour later they stomped into the kitchen, brushing snow from each other's coats.

"Have you heard from Higgins?" Miranda heard her grandma ask Mr. Taylor.

"He's out of the hospital and staying with his nephew. He's getting home nursing care."

"How is he?"

"He's healing nicely and as ornery as ever. I saw him last week, and he's chomping at the bit. The old race horse is determined to get back on track."

"A broken hip at his age can be hard to heal. I hope he recovers as well as he hopes," Grandpa said.

"It's all in the mind. The reason so many people don't recover is they give up. You won't see old Higgins giving up. He told me not to try to put him out to pasture. He may be an old horse, but he's a spirited one."

"I want to see him. Can we go to Bozeman to wish him Merry Christmas?" Miranda asked.

Grandpa looked at his watch and shook his head.

"Goodness! It's later than I thought. The afternoon has flown by. It's time to start milking, and I have to feed first. We'd better get going."

Miranda spent almost every day of vacation at Shady Hills Ranch. On the days that Chris and Laurie didn't go, Grandpa dropped her off, and she played with Elliot and cared for Starlight. When no one was around, she and Elliot would slip into Lady's stall. At first Elliot was reluctant to get on the mare, feeling he was deceiving his grandfather. *If Mr. Taylor would keep his promise, we wouldn't have to sneak around,* Miranda thought. She put an English bridle on Lady and showed Elliot how to turn her in the tiny stall.

"You are neck reining her, and she does fine that way, but you'd better learn to ride English, or your Grandfather won't be so happy."

"This is the way Mark taught me," Elliot said.

"I know. It's western. It's how I learned, too, and I like it best. Let me show you the way Adam taught Chris."

Elliot learned quickly and Lady responded to his light touch. To Miranda, it seemed that he became one with the mare when he rode her. There wasn't much teaching to be done, but Miranda did her best to pass on everything she'd heard Adam tell Chris. One day, Miranda opened the door to the paddock, told Elliot to duck his head, and led Lady into the winter air. Her ears pricked up, and she snorted but stood still as Elliot leaned forward to pat her neck.

"Let go of her," Elliot said. "I'll show you I can ride."

Miranda released the rein and stepped back. Elliot urged Lady forward with a shift of his weight. The horse responded immediately. Elliot allowed her to trot to the end of the paddock and turned to come back. He sat straight and proud and waved to Miranda as he held her to a walk along the paddock fence.

"Elliot! I hear a car coming!" Miranda shouted. Lady's paddock was in full view of the road where it topped the hill before the straight stretch down toward the cattle guard.

Chapter Twelve

School started all too soon for Miranda, but Elliot was happy to get back to his lessons. He said he couldn't wait to see Mark. Miranda hadn't seen much of him since the day she let him ride in the paddock. *I hope Mr. Taylor didn't see him on Lady.* But she dismissed the thought, sure that Mr. Taylor would have yelled at her if he had.

At school the Magnificent Four went on and on about the Winter Fair, the hotel they would stay in, and the shopping they planned to do in Bozeman.

"I have all new clothes for the show," said Kimberly, so loud the whole classroom could hear her. "I'm going to wear a blue silk western shirt, with silver trim on the pockets and a little diamond cut out in the back. I have black pants and new boots and a new black cowboy hat."

Miranda wondered if Grandma would make her wear her riding helmet during her performance. Chris and Laurie had helmets too, and Chris would look fine in his; it went with his English riding style. Miranda would feel like a real dork if she had to wear a helmet in the western trail event, especially since Laurie was getting a cowboy hat.

Miranda rode Elliot's bus to Shady Hills after school the first day after Christmas break. She sat across the aisle from him and Mark, and tried to break into his conversation. He didn't ignore her; Elliot was always polite, but somehow, he seemed more reserved than usual. Miranda was glad Mr. Taylor wasn't waiting at the bus stop. As they began walking she asked, "Are you mad at me?"

"No, I have no reason to be."

"Then why so quiet? You don't talk to me anymore."

Elliot sighed. "I'm afraid you will tell me I should ride Lady again, and I do want to ever so much."

"I just wanted to make your wish come true."

"I do wish it with all my heart. You said if I wished hard enough and long enough it would come true, but I wish for Grandfather to teach me. He's been very good to me, and I don't want to sneak rides behind his back."

"Oh, Elliot. You haven't done anything bad. I'd tell him it's my fault. He won't have trouble believing that!"

"What you do is your fault, and what I do is my fault. I know how I feel inside."

"Okay, okay! I don't want you to feel bad. I just think it stinks that you don't get to ride when you are so good at it, that's all." Miranda felt ashamed, and to cover it up, she became defensive. "I just thought it would be fun to surprise your grandfather when we show him. He'd be pleased to see how good you are, I think."

"You don't really think that, do you?" Elliot asked.

"Well, no. I guess not."

When Miranda came home from school just a week before the Winter Fair, she saw a package on the table. *It's just the right size for a cowboy hat*, she thought.

"Is this for me?" she asked.

"Yes, it's your Christmas gift from your mother. Do you want to open it now or wait until Grandpa comes in for supper?"

Miranda wanted to rip it open then and there, but it was a family tradition to share the joy of surprises, so she agreed to wait. She picked up the package and was surprised at the weight of it; too heavy for just a hat. *Maybe Mom put other things in with it*, she told herself as she set the table.

When Grandpa finally came in and washed up for supper, Miranda set the package beside her plate.

"Go ahead and open it," Grandpa said. "I want to see what you got."

Miranda tore off the brown paper and found the box sealed with heavy tape. Grandpa had to get out his pocket knife to open it. Inside were several brightly wrapped packages with labels, none of them big enough to hold a hat. She tried to hide her disappointment as she pulled the presents out of the box.

"This one's for you, Grandpa."

He opened it, and found a tri-fold leather wallet.

"All right! Did you tell her what I needed, Kathy?" he asked Grandma as he pulled his worn one from his pocket and began putting the contents into the new one.

"No, I didn't, but I'm glad she thought of it. When Corey and Jolene didn't give you one, I wished I had."

"Here's one for you," Miranda said, handing a heavy rectangular box to Grandma.

"Shower gel, bath oil, and a bottle of perfume! She must be trying to make me smell better," laughed Grandma. But Miranda could tell by Grandma's smile that she liked it.

There were three packages left, all for Miranda. She opened them slowly. One was a book called "Anne of Green Gables." From what she read on the back cover, it was about a girl who, like herself, was sent to live with people who were not her parents. *Another orphan! Is that the way Mom sees me, too?* The second box contained an assortment of fingernail polish. Miranda never painted her fingernails. She didn't even take time to trim or clean them unless she was reminded. The third box was the biggest and heaviest. Miranda opened it to find a silver box with a hinged lid. Opening it, she found two rings, a gold bracelet, and a pendant on a gold chain tucked into the red velvet-lined compartments.

"It's pretty," Miranda finally said, as she blinked back the tears that were stinging the corners of her eyes.

"Christmas must have cost your mom a lot of money. This jewelry is expensive, Miranda."

Maybe, but it shows that my mother doesn't know me.

Mrs. Langley, Laurie, and Miranda settled into the small room in the Rainbow Motel on North Seventh Avenue in Bozeman. It wasn't Bozeman's finest, but it was within walking distance of the fairgrounds, which is all Miranda cared about. She was anxious to get there to see if the Bergman's had arrived with Queen.

"I think I'll just start walking," Miranda said as she watched Mrs. Langley put her belongings neatly in drawers and on hangers in the closet.

"Oh, I'll be ready in just a few minutes. I thought we could go eat at Frontier Pies before we go to the fairgrounds. After all, you don't compete until tomorrow."

"I'm not really hungry. I'd rather go see if I can help Chris get Queen settled. You and Laurie go ahead and eat. I can walk, really."

"Just hold on a second, Miranda. I know Laurie isn't going to let you go alone," chuckled Mrs. Langley. "I'll drive you, get your fair buttons, and help you find the Bergmans."

Miranda saw Bergman's big Dodge pickup with the deluxe horse trailer pulling into the fairgrounds a few cars ahead of them. As soon as the buttons were pinned to their coats, Miranda and Laurie ran toward the horse barns. Chris was backing Queen out of the trailer. The mare sniffed the air and snorted, every muscle ready for action.

"She's as excited as I am to be here," Miranda called to Chris. "She probably smells the other horses. Which stall does she go into? Do you want me to lead her?"

"No, that's all right. I'll take her," Chris answered, tightening his grip on the lead-rope.

Miranda noticed a change in the relationship between Chris and his horse. The old fears seemed to be replaced by an affection that made him proud and possessive of the flashy sorrel thoroughbred.

"I'll help carry the equipment," Miranda offered.

"This box has all the brushes, combs, picks, shampoo,

and whatever other paraphernalia my wife could think of," Mr. Bergman said. "Maybe you and Laurie could each grab a handle."

"This is so exciting," Laurie squealed as they carried the wooden box to the barn behind Queen. "Look at all the horses. I never realized there would be so many. We have more to worry about than just the Magnificent Four."

"Don't worry, Laurie. Queen is probably better trained than any of them and prettier than most. And we can ride as well as anyone!" Miranda exclaimed.

"I hope you're right. I'm so nervous!"

Before English equitation the next morning, Queen was decked out in her English finery. Her sorrel coat and golden mane and tail glistened. Her warm breath clouded the brisk air.

"My knees are shaking, and it's not just from the cold," Chris said, as he prepared to mount.

"Don't worry. Just trust Queen and remember what Adam told you. Be sure to listen to the judge so you know when to walk, trot, or canter. It may not always be in that order." Miranda said.

"Yeah. just like in practice, right?" Chris said.

"Right, you both know what to do."

Miranda and Laurie watched him enter the arena with five other competitors. Once in the ring, his fear seemed to vaporize. He sat tall, looked straight ahead, and wore a smug smile. "Good thing he likes to show off; for once it's helping him," Miranda whispered to Laurie.

Finally the horses lined up side by side, and the judge

awarded ribbons. A blue and gold rosette on a long ribbon was placed around Queen's neck. Miranda bubbled with joy as she met Chris at the gate. He grinned at her as she gave him a thumbs up.

"Great job, son," Mr. Bergman said, as he and his wife approached. "But the next event's the hard one."

The hunter class began at one o'clock in the afternoon. Miranda stayed with Chris and Queen between the two events, pampering the horse and talking.

"Nervous?" Miranda asked.

"I'd say!" Chris exclaimed. "Especially with my parents watching."

"Forget about them. Pretend there's nobody but you and Queen in the whole world."

"Right now, I wish there wasn't—well, except for you, maybe." He smiled.

"Next up, Chris Bergman on Queen of Royal Flush." Chris's grin disappeared and he gulped.

"Remember—just you and Queen. Have fun!" Miranda shouted as he entered the arena.

Except for some pretty tight turns after a couple of the jumps, the course was easier than Adam's practice layout, where Chris had mastered higher jumps. He wouldn't be judged on time, just how well Queen performed. At one tight jump in the far corner, it looked like Chris lost his balance, but he quickly regained his seat. Miranda heard Chris's father say, "He's not very smooth." *I'd like to see you do as well,* she thought.

When all the riders were called back in to line up before

the judges, Christopher's name was announced last. He'd won first prize. When his parents stood and clapped, a smile spread across his face.

"Let's all go celebrate," offered Mr. Bergman. "Where would you like to go for a late lunch, Son?"

"McDonalds!" he exclaimed.

"McDonalds?" Mr. Bergman shouted. "You've got to be kidding. I'm not taking a winner to a fast food joint."

"But I like McDonalds," Chris argued. "I hardly ever get a chance to eat there."

"If we're honoring the winner, dear," Mrs. Bergman chided, "don't you think we should let the choice be his?" The finest dining could not have brought more joy to the three friends. As they chomped down hamburgers, they recounted every jump and maneuver, punctuating each one with high fives, knuckle punches, and exclamations like "way-to-go, Chris!" and "We knew you could do it."

Cars drove by on North Seventh Avenue until late into the night, keeping Miranda wide awake. When she finally dozed off a little after midnight, a siren screamed, jolting her awake again. Miranda was used to complete quiet when she slept with her bedroom window slightly ajar. She loved a cool breeze wafting past her nose as she snuggled warmly under a heavy comforter. The motel room was too warm, yet the heater came on noisily from time to time. It was after one o'clock before Miranda fell asleep.

She dreamed she rode a wild black stallion, her Starlight, running like the wind across an open meadow. But this time, the horse vanished from beneath her. She ran through dense trees and thick mud, calling for Starlight. She came to a rickety barn and saw Starlight's face—close up. His eyes were rimmed in white, and his flared nostrils were glowing red. His ears were pinned back as the rotting boards of the building began to fall. His terrified scream cut through her like a knife.

Jolting upright, drenched in sweat, Miranda slowly realized that the shriek that continued from her dream was coming from Laurie's alarm clock. Although she knew she'd only been dreaming, the nightmare was so vivid that she couldn't stop shaking. Throughout the day, she was haunted with the feeling that Starlight was in trouble and needed her help.

Chapter Thirteen

In contrast to her dream, the wintry Saturday morning was bright and clear. Laurie was scheduled to compete in Western Pleasure at 11:00. Miranda's trail class began at 2:00. Grandma and Grandpa would be there to watch.

Laurie looked beautiful in her new black Wranglers and western boots. Her dark hair was neatly French-braided in one long braid down her back. She wore a silver-grey felt cowboy hat that matched the tailored jacket, which she wore unbuttoned over a mauve satin blouse. She didn't seem the least bit nervous as she mounted Queen and rode into the arena. Kimberly rode a blood-bay quarter horse gelding. He had a white blaze and four white stockings. Kimberly sat tall in the saddle, her chin tilted upward and her face straight ahead.

Kimberly will be Laurie's toughest competitor, Miranda told herself as she watched the nine contestants ride around the arena, first at a walk, then a trot, breaking into a canter on command. Miranda looked at the panel of judges, knowing they would be watching carefully for the correct lead changes, noting how quickly the horses responded to their riders' cues. The riders were told to stop, back their horses, and do a side pass. "Canter," called the judge in the center of the ring. Queen immediately responded to Laurie's cues, going from walk to canter without a misstep or lead change. Kimberly's horse kicked at Queen as she passed, then he exploded into a run. Kimberly jerked back on the reins as her hat flew off her head. The bay took two jerky steps and then smoothed to an easy canter.

They were asked to come to a stop, side by side, facing the judge in the center of the ring. They all dismounted and stood to the left of their mount. The judge gave the riders ribbons, beginning with fifth place. Kimberly received the second place. Laurie got first. Tears filled Kimberly's eyes, and her face was red as she led her horse from the arena.

"This horse can do it all, it seems. Two ribbons under an English rider, and now first place for Western Pleasure," the announcer said as Laurie left the ring. "She'll be performing the trail class later today. You won't want to miss it." Queen seemed to strut as the crowd cheered.

"You did it!" Miranda said. "For a while it was so close I couldn't breathe. I'd better do as well. Tammy's sure she'll win the trail class like she did the last two years."

"She didn't win it year before last. She got a red ribbon. But she keeps telling everybody she won," Chris said. "Don't worry about it, Miranda. You can do everything they can possibly set up, and Queen is on a roll."

For lunch, they finally went to Frontier Pies with Laurie's Mom, but Miranda was so nervous she couldn't eat a bite. When they got back to the fairgrounds, Grandma and Grandpa were waiting at Queen's stall.

"It's been awfully quiet without you around the house," Grandpa said.

"Your chickens and bunnies look at me like I'm an alien when I feed them. We'll all be glad when you are home," Grandma added. "Are you having fun?"

"Oh, yes. This is so exciting. Gram, Laurie said I could wear her cowboy hat. Please let me. I think the judges will take points off if I'm wearing a helmet."

"Nonsense. You'll be judged on your performance, that's all."

"But what can happen? Queen is behaving perfectly. Everyone else wears a hat."

"The trail event is dangerous. There are too many things that could spook her; picking up that yellow slicker off the fence post and putting it on, leaning over to open and close the gate. That's where you got hurt before, remember?"

Miranda opened her mouth to protest, but the look in Grandma's eyes said, "don't bother." She nodded and looked again at the schedule.

"Oh, look, there's Higgins!" Chris shouted, grabbing Miranda's shoulder.

She turned to see Mr. Taylor pushing a wheel chair into the barn. Higgins smiled broadly as they approached. Elliot walked on one side and Higgins' nephew, John, on the other.

"Higgins!" Miranda squealed as she ran to the old man's side. "I'm so glad to see you. You don't look sick at all!"

"I'm not sick, never was," Higgins said, smiling at Miranda. "Can't let a little thing like a broken bone keep me down. I had to come see you win a blue ribbon."

"Thanks for coming, Mr. Higgins. I know she'll do her best," Grandma said.

"She always does," Higgins said, "but please just call me Higgins, or I'll be looking around to see who you're talking to. When are you up, Miranda?"

"A girl from Belgrade goes first, then Tammy, then a boy from Livingston. I'm after him. That means I can watch Tammy and the other girl and get an idea of the layout."

"I'll help you get Queen saddled and ready to go," offered Chris.

"We'll go find a good seat," said Grandpa.

Laurie stayed to help Chris and Miranda put the western saddle on Queen. Mr. Taylor followed her grandparents, pushing Higgins' wheel chair.

"I'm going to leave her in the stall long enough to go watch Tammy, then I'll bridle her and get in line," Miranda decided, anxious to join her grandparents. She had missed them more than she realized.

The course was similar to the one they had put together at Shady Hills. One difference was a three foot wide bridge that was made in an arch. The first rider's horse shied and went around it. The rider circled back and approached the bridge more slowly. The horse sidestepped a few times before it stepped onto it and hurried across. The girl got a deduction for dropping an envelope when her horse stepped away from the mail box too quickly. Tammy's horse, a lanky buckskin gelding, stepped onto the bridge and then jumped across. Miranda thought the judges gave a deduction for that, but wasn't sure. Tammy made no more mistakes that Miranda could see.

"That's going to be hard to beat. The only way I might do better is to make sure Queen walks across the bridge without jumping it," Miranda told Laurie and Chris as they made their way back to Queen's stall.

"Don't worry!" Chris said. "I've seen you ride. You're a heck of a lot better than Tammy. Did you see how awkward she looked when her horse hopped over the bridge?"

"Did you hear anything?" Miranda asked as she rounded the corner and peered into the empty alleyway. I thought I heard a stall door shut."

"Me too. And then someone running," Laurie said. "Probably the next rider hurrying to get to the arena."

"No, he was already waiting at the gate. I better hurry and get there myself." Miranda bridled Queen and led her from the stall. Queen stumbled, but regained her footing and followed.

"She sure is acting funny," Laurie commented as Miranda tightened the cinch.

"Yeah, maybe she's tired," Miranda said as she mounted and patted the mare's neck. "Never mind, Queen, just one more contest, and then we'll take you home to rest."

"And now, Miranda Stevens on Queen of Royal Flush," boomed a deep voice over the loudspeaker.

Miranda urged Queen forward, but she barely moved. Miranda had to kick her in the ribs before she stepped forward. Queen took three faltering steps into the arena and fell to her knees. As if in slow motion, she let her hips sink and rolled slowly to her side. Miranda kicked free of the stirrups, and stood beside Queen as she stretched her neck out on the ground and closed her eyes.

A gasp and then a roar went up from the crowd.

"Somebody get a vet!" Miranda screamed. "Quick!"

"Is there a veterinarian in the building?" asked the announcer, but there was already a man kneeling beside the mare.

"I'm Dr. Anderson. Are you the owner?"

"I am!" shouted Chris. "What happened? Is she dead?"

"She's not breathing, but she still has a pulse," the vet replied, reaching into his bag.

There were tears in Chris's eyes as he fell to his knees beside the horse and tried to hug her neck. People swarmed around them, all talking at once. A familiar voice reached Miranda's ears. "Jeez, Miranda, that's one way to get out of competing with me. Maybe she took one look at your ugly helmet and fainted."

Miranda, overcome with rage, wheeled and grabbed Tammy by her fancy shirt.

"You did this, didn't you? You don't have the guts to win fair and square! You didn't think you could beat me, so you poisoned my horse—Chris's horse! If she dies, I hope you go to prison for life. That's the lowest, meanest thing in the world. I should beat..."

"Stop it. Miranda, I didn't do anything!" Tammy shouted, pulling away.

"Miranda, calm down. Beating up on Tammy won't help Queen. Come on, the vet needs room to work. They're trying to clear the arena, and you aren't helping," said Grandpa.

Miranda let go of Tammy and turned back to Queen.

Chris was on his feet now, standing behind the veterinarian. Dr. Anderson gave Queen a shot with a big syringe. Mr. and Mrs. Bergman looked on. "She's been given a pretty strong paralytic drug; a form of curare, as far as I can tell. The lab report from a blood sample will tell us for sure. I gave her Neostigmine to reverse the effects. If I'm right, she'll be on her feet in ten minutes or so. Look, she's coming around."

Sure enough, Queen's eyes were opening, and she raised her head enough to survey the crowd with a bewildered look in her eyes.

"What's curare?" asked Miranda.

"It's a concoction prepared by South American Indians to make poison arrows. In smaller doses, forms of it are used as a muscle relaxant along with anesthesia and to treat certain diseases in both animals and humans."

Queen laid her head back on the ground for a few long seconds and then struggled to her feet.

"I want to ride home with you," Miranda told Grandpa an hour later. "Bergmans are taking Queen home."

"Before you go, there's something you should know," said Tammy. Stephanie, Lisa, and Kimberly stood beside her, forming a wall. "I would never do anything to hurt a horse no matter who it belonged to. I love horses."

Miranda didn't want to hear anything from Tammy.

"She's telling the truth, Miranda. We all love horses, but Tammy more than anyone," Lisa said. "None of us did anything to Chris's horse. But we think we know who did." Kimberly and Stephanie nodded.

"Who?" Miranda demanded.

"When I went back to put my horse away, I saw a man I'd never seen before hanging around the barn Queen was in," Tammy said. "He stepped around the corner when he saw us, like he was hiding."

"What did he look like?"

"Tall, wearing dark clothes—scary looking."

"Were his shoulders hunched? Did he have a little beard, just on his chin?"

"Yeah, I think so. He had a hat pulled down almost to his eyes. A stocking cap—a black one."

Chapter Fourteen

"Can't you drive faster, Grandpa?" Miranda asked as they cruised down Interstate 90 at what seemed like a snail's pace to her.

"What's your hurry? He's going the speed limit," Grandma said.

"I know who gave Queen the poison. He'll try to kill Starlight next. We have to get there before he does."

"Aren't you letting your imagination run away with you again, Miranda?" Grandpa asked, "Why would anyone want to kill Starlight?"

"It's Martin Hicks, and he hates me. He hates me AND Starlight."

"Do you mean the man Mr. Taylor hired after Higgins got hurt? You ran away with Starlight because you thought Mr. Taylor was going to get rid of the horse when he only intended to fire Mr. Hicks," Grandma recalled. "You have a tendency to worry about things that aren't really happening. Why would anyone hate you enough to hurt a couple of horses to get even? It makes no sense."

"He probably thinks it's my fault Mr. Taylor fired him. Mostly, I think he hates me because I can handle Starlight and he couldn't."

"I seriously doubt that he injected Queen; he has no reason to. But if he did, he's not likely to stick around and get caught," said Grandpa

Miranda hoped he was right, but she would put nothing past the meanness of Martin Hicks.

"Aren't you going to let me off at Shady Hills?" Miranda asked as they turned down the road toward home.

"Not now, Miranda. I'm late with chores as it is. I need your help getting the cows in and feeding while Grandma and I get set up and start milking," Grandpa said.

"But what about Starlight?" Miranda asked in dismay. "Mr. Hicks has had plenty of time to get there. I have to know if Starlight is okay!"

"Like I said before, I don't think there's any danger. But if it will make you feel better, call Mr. Taylor before you go get the cows."

Miranda ran to the house and grabbed the phone. Mr. Taylor wasn't home. He probably wouldn't come back from Bozeman until late. She called again and let it ring, hoping someone would hear the phone in the tack shed, but after a dozen rings she gave up.

Her grandparents were already working in the barn, so she set out on foot to round up the cows. There really was nothing to it, for as soon as they saw her open the gate to the corral, they hurried through and crowded around the barn door. Warmth and grain awaited them inside. Miranda closed the gate behind them and hurried inside to dole out grain at each stanchion. Then she filled a bucket of grain to take to the older calves in the feed lot. She fed the chickens and her bunnies in record time, not stopping to talk or cuddle them as she usually did.

When her chores were finally done, she hurried back to the house to call Shady Hills again. Still no answer. She called the Bergman's

"Hello?" Mrs. Bergman sounded out of breath.

"Hello. This is Miranda. Is Chris there?"

"We just walked in the door. I'll put him on."

"Chris, were you at Shady Hills?"

"Sure. We took Queen back. Doc Talbot met us there. He gave her another shot of something, but he says he thinks she'll be all right. They got the lab report back and there was enough of that curare stuff in her blood to kill her. She'd be dead if Dr. Anderson hadn't given her a shot when he did. Adam said he'd stay there tonight and keep an eye on her."

"Oh, good. I hope he'll keep an eye on Starlight, too. Did you see him? Is he okay?"

"Who, Adam?"

"No, Starlight."

"I didn't go look at him, but I suppose he's fine. Adam was there when we got there. He'd just finished the afternoon feeding."

"Oh, then he's probably all right."

"What's your problem? Why are you so worried about Starlight? Queen's the one who could die!" Chris said.

"I'm worried about her, too, Chris. I hope she gets well. If she doesn't, well, it's my fault, because if he hadn't known I was the one who would be riding her, he probably wouldn't have done it."

"Who? I don't know what you're talking about."

"Martin Hicks. He worked for Mr. Taylor for a little while, and he tried to get rid of Starlight then. I think he hates me because Mr. Taylor fired him instead of killing Starlight. I'm sure he'll try to kill Starlight, too."

"Jeez, maybe we should call the cops!"

"It wouldn't do any good. They wouldn't listen to a kid. I told my grandparents, and they won't do anything about it. They think it's my imagination."

"Well, I'm going to tell someone. If he did it, I want him to pay. It was my horse!"

Sunday dawned bright and sunny. Mrs. Bergman agreed to take Chris and Miranda to Shady Hills right after breakfast. Queen stretched her neck over the dutch door and nickered for oats as they stepped out of the minivan. Miranda ran to Starlight's stall. To her relief, he greeted her just as eagerly.

"Here's an apple for you, Starlight. I'm glad to see you're all right. I was so afraid something would happen to you, I could hardly sleep last night."

"Why were you worried about him?" asked Adam Barber from behind her.

"Oh, hi," Miranda stammered. "How long have you been standing there?"

"I just came out of the next stall. I'm getting the cleaning done early so I can go get some sleep. I stayed in Queen's stall last night and didn't sleep very well myself," Adam said.

"But why are you worried about Sir Jet? Queen is the one whose life was on the line."

"I'm afraid the same person who hurt Queen will try the same thing on Starlight."

"Whoever did this to Queen is probably in the next state by now. If he gets caught, he'll be in big trouble."

"You don't know how much he hates me."

"You think someone did this because he hates you? That's kind of egotistical, isn't it?"

"You don't like me, do you?" Miranda accused.

"Now why do you say that? Can you think of any reason why I wouldn't like you?"

"No, but you treat me like I have the plague. I don't know why."

"I guess I have been a little short with you. I didn't mean to hurt your feelings, and I didn't slight you consciously. When I heard how you horse-napped Sir Jet, took him to a cave in the mountains in the middle of the winter, in the middle of the night, no less, well, I had to admire you. That's when I realized that I've been hard on you, and I've been trying to make it up to you."

"You could start by telling me why you acted that way."

"Well, I'm not really sure. Tag along while I work, and I'll explain it the best I can."

"Sure. I'll get a pitchfork and help you."

"It's your eyes," Adam began as they mucked out the next stall. "I couldn't look into your big green eyes or gray or whatever color they are, without getting a lump in my throat, so I'd look away or do something else."

"What's wrong with my eyes? Grandma says they change colors with my mood, but I didn't think that was a bad thing."

"It's not a bad thing. Your eyes are beautiful. The problem is, my best friend had eyes just like yours, and whenever I see you, I'm reminded of him."

"Where is he? Did something happen to him?"

"He's dead. It's a long sad story, but maybe it's time I told somebody." Adam stopped working, a faraway look in his eyes. "We were in the navy together. He was hard to get acquainted with. Seemed like he was carrying around a deep sadness or something. After we became friends, he still wouldn't talk about it; just joked around and changed the subject if I asked him.

"Then one night there was an awful storm. We were on an aircraft carrier, somewhere in the middle of the Atlantic headed for the Persian Gulf. I never saw waves so big. They were crashing over the deck one second, then we'd be looking straight up at the lightning in the clouds the next, just to get slammed down into another huge trough again. That night after the storm came up, I actually saw Barry crying. This time he didn't try to cover up his feelings. While we sat there on that big deck watching waves the size of mountains, he told me what was eating him.

"He said he married the girl he'd fallen in love with when he went to high school in Montana. They got married right after graduation and the next thing he knew she was telling him she was pregnant. He said it took him by surprise, and he wasn't ready to be a father yet. He didn't think it could be his kid because it was so soon. They had a big fight and he left and joined the navy the next day. In no time at all, he was sorry. He wanted to go back, but the navy shipped him out. He said he wasn't sure why he never wrote or called her.

"I convinced him he'd feel better if he'd write her a letter. So that's what he did right there in the middle of the storm. He never quite finished it because..." Adam swallowed. "I'm not sure how it happened," he finally went on, "but there was a big explosion. Something slammed against a tank of jet fuel, I think. Fire broke out. You'd think the waves washing over the ship would have put it right out, but it was too big. Some of the crew had been right next to it. There was this one guy running around like a human torch. Barry tossed me the letter and yelled, 'Guard this with your life!' Then he ran and tackled the guy. He tried to smother the flames by rolling him on the deck, but the ship took another nose dive and they both slid off the edge. We threw out lifelines and lowered a lifeboat but it was no use in the heavy sea. The navy had choppers out looking for them for days, but no one ever saw either of them again."

"His name was Barry? What was his last name?"

"Stevens. Seaman Barrett Randolph Stevens. He was given a medal of honor in a memorial service, but his body was never recovered."

"My dad," Miranda murmured as her head began to spin, and she slid into darkness.

"I'm sorry." The voice came from far away. Her father was telling her he was sorry! With her eyes still closed she tried to raise her hand to touch him.

"Miranda, I'm so sorry," repeated the deep voice as a rough hand took hers and gently held it. "I didn't know for sure that he was your father, but the more I watched you, the more I suspected it. You are like him in so many ways."

She opened her eyes and looked into the brown eyes of Adam Barber.

"I should've thought of how you'd feel. I should have broken it to you easier, but like I said, I wasn't sure. He told me he lived in a small town in Montana. I didn't know the name of it or what part of the state it was in. The address the navy had for him was somewhere in Michigan. I guess that's where he grew up.

"I hung on to the letter he gave me, but there was no address on it. That's why I came to Montana when I got out of the service. I've been traveling around working here and there, looking for a tall blonde woman named Carey Stevens. For some reason, I was looking for a little boy, although Barry said he never found out whether his child was a boy or girl or if it even lived."

"You have a letter from my Dad?"

"I do. Tucked away in a locked box at home, along with his picture and his medal of honor. If it's okay with your grandmother, I'll take you home and we can stop by my trailer on the way and get it."

Chapter Fifteen

Miranda went to bed early, refusing any supper, but clinging to the letter as if her life depended on it. Adam was still in the living room, explaining everything to Grandma and Grandpa. "May I have your daughter's address?" he was saying when Miranda dashed in.

"Adam. I'm glad you're still here. Will you please stay with Starlight tonight?"

"What? No! I'm sleeping in my own bed tonight. Why?"

"He'll come when no one's around. If you can't, I want to. I can take my sleeping bag…"

"Miranda, stop that nonsense," Grandma said. "You aren't going anywhere. Please get the idea that Mr. Hicks is a threat to Starlight out of your head."

Miranda could hardly speak for the lump in her throat, and she couldn't keep the tears from falling. "Will you please check on him before you go to bed? Call me if he's, uh, not okay?"

"You are certainly a paranoid little girl, aren't you?"

Adam said, rolling his eyes and shaking his head. "Mr. Taylor's home. I'd think that would be enough to rest your mind."

"Mr. Taylor will be asleep in the house. That wouldn't keep Hicks from sneaking in."

"Okay, okay. I'll swing by there. If it'll make you feel better, I'll park my pickup in front of Sir Jet's stall and borrow the ranch truck to drive home."

"Would you? Oh thank you. That'll probably keep him away."

"Just this once, because I feel like I owe you. But I agree with your grandmother. I don't think Starlight's in any danger."

Miranda saw the look of pity, or was it scorn, in Adam's eyes. *He's saying this to humor me. I hope he'll really do it.* She went back to her room to cry alone.

Grandma and Grandpa came in after Adam left. "Mandy, I'm sorry if I embarrassed you in front of Adam. I know you're worried about Starlight. I'm sure he'll be all right with Adam's truck there," Grandma said as Grandpa held her hand. Miranda couldn't help it; she sobbed as Grandma hugged her.

"Have you read the letter?" Grandpa asked.

"Not yet," she said as she wiped her eyes. "I'll read it later."

She cried herself to sleep, still clutching the letter and her dad's picture. When she awoke hours later, she turned on the light, unfolded the letter, and smoothed out the wrinkles. This is what she read:

My dearest Carey,

I was so wrong to leave you like I did. I acted on impulse like I always do. Most of all I regret the terrible things I said to you. I can't believe I was so mean. I had no reason to doubt you. I was just scared. I didn't think I could be a good enough father. Now I wish I had the chance, and I hope I will someday. If you'll forgive me and take me back, I will come home to you and our little one as soon as I get out of the navy and this stupid war. You are everything to me, Carey. I think of you every waking moment. I dream of you all night. Someday, I will make it up to you, if I'm not too late.

Now just a note to our child:

Dear Son or Daughter,

You may think it's not possible for me to love someone I never met, but I love you. If I have my way, I'll come home and be the best dad any kid ever had. You've got to be a wonderful person if you're anything like your mother. And if you're anything like me, well, try to control that quick temper and your impulse to act before you think. I can't wait to...

There was no more. Miranda, who had thought she had cried all the tears her body could hold, began crying all over again. Finally she whispered, "My Daddy loved me," and fell asleep.

Miranda woke early the next morning. She dressed quickly and hurried outside. She felt as if she had changed overnight, and she wasn't ready to face people yet. She did her chores mechanically as she tried to analyze her new feelings.

"It's not just the sadness, because there's happiness, too," she told the chickens as she poured grain into their feeders. "I'm glad to know about my dad. I'm glad he was good and brave, and most of all, I'm glad he loved me. Even though he never met me, he knew what I'm like, because I'm like him."

She picked Patches up and cuddled him as she thought out loud. "I know what it is! I've found a part of me that was lost. I always felt like I wasn't quite a whole person; like I didn't completely know who I was. Now I do. I'm not different. It's just that I can name the parts of me now."

Putting Patches back and scratching Mopsy behind her long ears she thought of all the times people would say, "You have your mother's long legs," or "her dimple," or "Your mother had hair just like this when she was your age." Now she knew that she had some of her dad's qualities as well. His beautiful eyes, his straight nose and, best of all, his spirit. She was no longer confused by her quick temper and her way of jumping into things without thinking. Knowing where those traits came from made her feel all right about herself.

"Are you okay, Miranda?" Grandma asked when she sat

down to breakfast. "If you don't feel like going to school today, I'll write an excuse for you to stay home."

"No, I'm okay, Gram. But thanks. And if you want to read my dad's letter, it's under my pillow."

"Thanks, Mandy," Grandma said, reaching for her hand and looking into her eyes. "I called your mom last night. Grandpa and I thought she should know right away, even though Adam wanted to break it to her in person. She was awfully upset, but wants to know more about it. I'm sure she'll want to talk to you later." Grandma drew a deep breath. "Adam wants to take the letter and go see her. He thinks that might make it easier for her."

"No, I want to keep the letter," Miranda paused, afraid she sounded selfish. "I mean, what if he loses it?"

"He hasn't lost it after all these years; I don't think he will now, but it's an easy matter to photocopy it. You can keep the original," Grandma added, stopping Miranda's protest. "Adam called while you were outside. He said to tell you he just got to work, and Starlight is fine."

Maybe Adam's not so bad after all, Miranda thought.

Mrs. Bergman drove Chris, Laurie, and Miranda to Shady Hills after school to check on the horses.

The ranch seemed deserted when they got there. Mr. Taylor had gone to a horse sale and wouldn't be back until late. Who knew where Adam was? Elliot had gone to the Wagner's to play with Mark after school.

Queen seemed to be feeling fine, and they decided to take her out and ride her a little.

"Just around the arena a few times. I've got to get back home," said Mrs. Bergman. "I'm entertaining tonight, and I don't quite have everything ready."

"You two ride Queen, and I'll lead Starlight around the arena with you," said Miranda.

"You can ride first, Laurie," offered Chris. He walked beside Miranda and Starlight as Queen pranced ahead.

"Time to put them up now," Mrs. Bergman called when they had circled the arena twice.

"Mom, I didn't get to ride yet!" Chris complained.

"Chris, no arguments, please," Mrs. Bergman said. "You do want to come again, don't you?"

Miranda put Starlight back in his stall and helped Chris put Queen's tack away. Looking across the barren fields Miranda could see the grain elevator towering above other buildings in town. Tumbleweeds filled the fence that divided Mr. Taylor's field from the schoolyard. The willows that lined the small creek along the field's north boundary swayed in the wind as low clouds scudded across the sky. A sudden chill shook Miranda's body as a feeling of foreboding swept over her.

"I'm going to stay awhile. Grandma will come and get me," Miranda told Mrs. Bergman.

"Well, if that's all right with her," Mrs. Bergman replied, starting the mini-van. "Just promise you won't ride."

"I won't, I promise," Miranda said and hurried back to Starlight. "I'll just stay until Mr. Taylor gets back. Maybe he'll listen to me and keep watch over you," Miranda told Starlight as she brushed his shining coat. "It's still early, Grandma won't be worrying."

Starlight began nibbling on hay, and Miranda sat in the corner of his stall to watch. He was becoming stronger everyday. Dr. Talbot seemed to think he would be able to walk without a limp, maybe even run, once the cast came off. She had overheard the veterinarian tell Mr. Taylor that it was nothing short of a miracle that the tendon wasn't severed when everything else was cut so deeply. She wondered when they'd take the cast off. She could hardly wait to try riding him. Maybe she could do it now, but no, she wouldn't risk hurting him again.

Her thoughts turned to her father. She hadn't asked Adam when he had died. *How long had he been in the navy?* she wondered. If only she had gotten a letter from him years ago, maybe she could have written back, or if she was too little, at least her mother would have known that he still loved her. *Oh, well. Better now than never.*

Starlight's head went up, and he rumbled deep in his throat. Miranda tensed and jumped to her feet as a dark form came through the door and lunged at Starlight. Frozen in fear, she watched Starlight rise on his hind legs and knock a man to the floor. Rolling quickly out of the way of the pounding hooves, Martin Hicks jumped to his feet just inches from Miranda.

"You!" he yelled. "This is good. I can get rid of both of you at the same time. It won't take much to make it look like your precious horse trampled you to death," he said as he shoved her into the path of the enraged stallion. "Then they'll wish they'd listened to me!"

Miranda met Starlight's rising foreleg and was flung back against Hicks, who pushed her forward again. Starlight stopped, and reaching over Miranda's head, he sunk his teeth into Martin Hicks' arm.

"Let go, you devil!" Hicks screamed.

Starlight lifted the man off his feet and shook him before dropping him in a heap. Hicks's hand fell on a syringe where he had dropped it when Starlight bit him. Gripping it, he rose to his knees and plunged it into Starlight's chest. Starlight reared and struck out with both feet, shaking the needle loose. Miranda saw the syringe dangle from Starlight's skin and then fall into a depression where Starlight's

hooves had scraped the shavings off the floor. It rested, needle end up against the shavings.

Hicks dodged the sharp hooves and scrambled to his feet, only to meet Starlight's knee with his face. Falling backward, he landed on the syringe. Starlight came down on the man's shoulder, then rose up again on his hind legs.

"Starlight, no! Easy, boy," Miranda shouted, jumping in front of the rearing stallion.

Starlight dropped back down to all fours without touching her and stood, shaking. He sniffed the inert body on the floor. Miranda opened the back door, and Starlight darted from the stall to the far end of his paddock. Hicks didn't move as Miranda scooted past him and ran to the tack shed. She grabbed the phone, called Doctor Talbot and then 911. The operator asked her to stay on the line, but after giving them directions to the ranch, she hung up and called Grandma.

The answering machine picked up. *They must be out doing chores.* "Grandma, please come get me at Shady Hills. There's been an accident." Miranda couldn't think of anything else to say that wasn't too complicated for a brief message. She ran back to the stall. Stopping at the door, she peered in. Hicks still lay on the stable floor. His arm and shoulder looked mangled and out of place. She walked around him, keeping as far away as she could for fear he would wake up and grab her. He moaned.

"Help," he said, feebly. He was staring straight at her with wild, wide-open eyes. She measured the distance to the door, ready to run.

"Please!" he screamed. "Get it out of me!"

Miranda hesitated, wondering what he was talking about. "Please," he whined again, "I can't reach it."

Miranda stepped nearer as the man, holding his mangled arm and shoulder, slowly rolled away from her, yelping in pain as he moved. Then she saw it. The syringe lifted off the floor, the tip of the needle lodged in his hip.

"Get it out, please," he cried. Miranda reached down, grasped the syringe, and pulled it free as she jumped back out of his reach. "Aw. Thank you. Is it empty?" Hicks asked, rolling back over. The barrel of the syringe was about a fourth full.

"Not quite," she said. "How much was in it?"

The man's eyes closed, and he didn't answer. Miranda ran to her beloved horse.

"Starlight, please be all right. Don't keel over like Queen did. I hope you got rid of that awful syringe in time."

Starlight snorted as she approached. His ears were forward, and his whole body seemed spring-loaded for action. As she reached her hand out to stroke him, he quivered but gradually relaxed as she patted his neck.

Chapter Sixteen

The eerie wail of a siren reached Miranda's ears, and she could see flashing red and blue lights a mile away on the county road. They soon disappeared from sight behind the hills on the winding lane that led to the stables. When they appeared again, it looked like a parade. First came the sheriff's Suburban, lights and siren still on, followed by an ambulance, Doctor Talbot's truck, Mr. Taylor's Cadillac, and, last of all, Grandma's Subaru. Miranda gently stroked Starlight as she looked him over for any sign that he was drugged. He seemed as alert as she was, watching the procession cross the cattle guard.

When Miranda entered the stall, the medics from the ambulance were leaning over Martin Hicks' still form.

"There's a faint heartbeat but his blood pressure's low. Let's get him to the hospital quick."

"Watch that arm! Here, let's slide him onto this board from the other side. Yeah, that's the way. Put his arm over his chest and let's snug him down."

Miranda was amazed at how quickly they had him

strapped down on a stretcher with an oxygen mask clamped over his nose and mouth. As soon as Hicks was inside, the ambulance started up the lane. Before they topped the first hill the lights were flashing and the siren screaming. The sheriff started to follow, then stopped and came back.

"Where's Starlight?" asked Doc Talbot.

"At the end of the paddock. I'll show you."

"Oh no, you don't, Miranda. Let me look at you!" Grandma sounded terrified, and Miranda turned around.

"Don't worry, I'll find the horse. You'd better let your Grandmother look after you," Dr. Talbot said.

"Grandma, I'm fine. I need to make sure Starlight's going to be all right."

"Miranda, what happened to you?" Grandma asked holding her tightly by the arm and staring at her face.

"What do you mean?"

"Your face is skinned, and your hair is full of shavings. Is that blood on your chin?" Grandma touched her face and looked at her finger. "No, just a little horse manure. But your face is swollen and red."

Miranda touched her face and was amazed at the sharp sting she felt. She hadn't realized that she had been hurt in the commotion. When she felt a throbbing pain in her shoulder, she remembered meeting Starlight's foreleg and being thrown back against Hicks. There had been so much excitement, she hadn't felt anything but fear and anger.

"Bring her into the house and clean her up, if you want, Kathy," offered Mr. Taylor.

"Oh, please, not yet. I'm fine. It hardly hurts at all. I've gotta check on Starlight!"

"Don't worry about him. I'll help the vet," said Grandpa, who had left his milking to come with Grandma.

Grandma led her into the house. Elliot and Mr. Taylor were right behind them. With a warm wash cloth, Grandma sponged her cheek.

"Ouch," Miranda yelped, jumping back.

She stared into the bathroom mirror at her reddened cheek and blackened eye, amazed. Maybe Starlight's hoof had struck her.

"Please tell me everything that happened," Grandma said, guiding Miranda back to the kitchen, brushing her tangled hair.

"I want to hear it, too," said the sheriff, stepping in the back door.

As Miranda told the story, Grandma slumped into a chair. When she got to the part about pulling the syringe from Hicks, the sheriff said, "Ah, we found the syringe. It's on it's way to the lab for analysis. How much was in it to start with, did you see?"

Miranda shook her head. "No, I asked him, but he passed out before he could answer."

"You're going to be the death of me, child," Grandma said tenderly. "You were right about the danger to Starlight, and we didn't think you were. But, I wish you wouldn't keep taking things into your own hands. If you'd called me when the Bergman's left, I could have been here before Mr. Hicks."

"If you had, he would've seen your car and waited. You would have taken me home, while he came back and killed Starlight. Now they have him, and he won't be hurting any more horses." Miranda added, "He might even die."

"It isn't well to wish death on anyone. Like everyone else, he'll have to reap the consequences of his actions." With a shudder Grandma pulled Miranda close and hugged her. "He would have murdered you if Starlight hadn't knocked him down first."

"Wow, Miranda, what a shiner!" Josh said as she entered the classroom the next morning. "It must be true what they're saying about you. Is that how you got the black eye?"

"What are they saying?" Miranda asked.

"That you captured that horse-killer," another boy exclaimed. "You have all the excitement."

"And close calls!" exclaimed Laurie. "I hope you live long enough to start a horse ranch with me."

Miranda was surprised that word had gotten out so quickly. "Dad saw it on the ten o'clock news, last night," Josh said. "It was in the Montana Standard this morning," added Laurie.

Miranda answered eager questions until Mrs. Penrose interrupted. "Take your seats, everyone. We'll have Miranda come up front and tell the whole class what happened."

At lunch time, the Magnificent Four approached Miranda, Chris, and Laurie in the cafeteria. "We decided we should all be friends," Kimberly announced. "You can join our riding club. We'll even let Laurie and Miranda ride our horses since you don't have any of your own."

"Just like that?" Laurie asked, her face turning red. "Just because Miranda is suddenly famous, and you know she wouldn't join your club without me, you expect me to consider it a privilege to be your friend?"

Miranda was astonished at the anger in her friend's voice. It was so unlike her. Kimberly looked as if someone had just slapped her.

"I...no, that's not the reason. I was just trying to be nice," Kimberly stammered.

"Well, don't try. If you can't like me for who I am, if it's so hard to 'be nice' to a 'nigger,' then stay away from me, and I won't bother you."

"Look, I'm really sorry," Kimberly said.

"Laurie, we were real jerks to you—and to Chris and Miranda, too. We're sorry," said Lisa. "I know how you feel and..."

"You have no idea how I feel," Laurie interrupted. "You don't think I have feelings. Just because my grandmother is black, you suppose I'm some subspecies that doesn't experience the same feelings you do. I suppose you think my grandmother has no more brains or feelings than a, a..."

"Wait. No. I never thought that! I guess I didn't really think about how you felt," said Tammy. "I'm sorry."

"I didn't mean I'm trying to be nice. I mean I really want to be friends. I don't blame you if you won't after all the mean things we said, but I hope you will," said Kimberly.

"What about Chris and Miranda? You said terrible things about them, too," Laurie accused.

"Sorry, Chris," Stephanie said. "I promise not to call you 'fat boy' again."

"Miranda, I'm sorry I called you 'orphan,'" Lisa said.

"Maybe I am an orphan. I don't have a father because he died trying to save someone's life," Miranda said. "I do have a mother, but I don't think it's any of your business if she wants me to live with my grandparents right now. I like living with them. I'm not ashamed of being an orphan, but I think it's stupid to hate people for their skin or body type or who they live with."

"Okay. We get the point, and I agree. Can't we all be friends?" asked Tammy.

"Since we don't have to practice for the horse show anymore, you could come over to my house after school," offered Kimberly. "I have a horse we can use to pull a sled. We can take turns."

"I wouldn't dare go to your house, Kimberly," said Laurie. "I know what your parents think of my dad. They would probably tell me to get off their property."

"Well, they're wrong. I know that now. When I saw you ride, well, after I got over being mad about you winning, I realized we're a lot alike. We both love horses, and we both ride well. I thought we could be friends."

"If you really mean it, I'm sure we can," said Laurie. "Sorry I got so mad. It just hurts when people think they're so much better than me."

Miranda was surprised to see Grandma's car when school let out for the day. "Grandma, what are you doing here? Are you taking us to Shady Hills?"

"No, I'm taking you home. I'm just on my way back from Bozeman."

"But I want to see Starlight."

"And I want you to rest. You've had enough excitement for a while." Miranda started to argue, but realized she was awfully tired—and sore.

Grandma suggested a warm bath for her sore muscles and told her to rest. She even did Miranda's chores for her. After a relaxing bath, Miranda lay down, but couldn't sleep as yesterday's events swirled like a cyclone through her mind. She noticed the book Mom had given her for Christmas lying on her dresser and opened it for the first time. There, just inside the front cover in her Mom's neat handwriting were these words:

> My Dearest Miranda,
>   This was my favorite book when I was your age. I wish we could read it together, but since we can't, would you call me after you read some of it? That way we can enjoy talking about it.
>   Love always, Mom

Miranda sighed, imagining how Mom must have felt when she hadn't called; hadn't even thanked her.

"Are you going to Shady Hills today, Chris?" Miranda asked when the final bell rang the next day.

"No, can't today. Mom's going to Dillon and wants me to go. I have some cousins I haven't seen for awhile."

"Can your mother take us?" she asked Laurie.

"I think she's planning on it. It's her turn, and even though we aren't practicing for anything, I told her we want to see how Queen and Starlight are doing," answered Laurie. "Have you heard anything about the guy who tried to kill them?"

"No, not yet. Mr. Taylor probably knows."

Miranda was in a hurry as she walked to Laurie's house, but Laurie walked slowly and kept stopping to look at things. Mrs. Langley wasn't ready when they got there. Miranda was about to burst with impatience. A half hour later, looking like she had just stepped out of a beauty shop, Laurie's mom announced that she was ready to go.

As they pulled into the drive between the stable and the tack shed, Miranda saw Elliot in the round pen on a horse!

Unable to believe her eyes, she jumped out of the car and ran to the fence.

"Elliot, what horse is that you're riding? Does Mr. Taylor know?"

"Of course he does!" Elliot said with a triumphant smile. "You were right, Miranda. I kept wishing, and my wish came true. This is Sunny. She's the mother to Chris's Queen. Her real name is Sundance Queen, and she's twelve years old."

"But I thought you weren't allowed to ride."

Elliot expertly reined the mare to the fence where Miranda was climbing over. He stopped Sunny and looked down at Miranda.

"I couldn't keep the secret inside anymore. I had to tell Grandfather what we did," Elliot said softly. "I hope you aren't mad at me for telling our secret."

"No, of course not, but what did he say? Is he mad?"

"He was angry at first, but then he wanted to see me ride, so he saddled up this horse and told me to ride in here. He watched me and said I ride well."

"Wow!" Miranda said, shaking her head. "Why aren't you riding Lady?"

"Grandfather sold her because she isn't going to have a foal for the second year in a row. Sunny won't this year either, but he's keeping her anyway. Here he comes."

Chapter Seventeen

Mr. Taylor looked angry as he strode down the lane from the indoor arena.

"So, you've been up to your old tricks," he said gruffly, scowling at Miranda. "Not only riding horses that don't belong to you..."

"I didn't ride," Miranda started to argue, but when Mr. Taylor held up his hand, she stopped.

"Teaching little boys to do so is even worse. You ought to be ashamed of yourself," Mr. Taylor continued. "Are you?"

"But Mr. Taylor, you didn't have time to teach him, and I knew how much he wanted..."

"Answer my question!"

"I...I guess, I mean, well, yes...we, I mean, I should've asked you first. But I knew you'd say no," Miranda stuttered. "Wouldn't you?"

"You still think I'm a mean old man, don't you?" Mr. Taylor asked. "I only want the best for Elliot, though I don't suppose you believe that. But no matter what you think of me, or what you thought I'd answer, you have no right to take my business and my property into your own hands."

Miranda looked down, suddenly feeling ashamed.

"I'm sorry," she muttered.

"I have to say, though, you did a good job of teaching him. I was afraid he'd learn to ride like some of these farm kids I see in the neighborhood. Elliot rides like a feather in his English saddle. I had to show him how to use that, though. I'd never have started out teaching him to ride bareback."

"I don't see anything wrong with bareback or western riding. I think it's good to know them and English, too," Miranda said.

"You always have your opinions, don't you? Well, you'd better go see to Sir Jet. He's looking for you. Just don't be messing with any of the other horses without asking. Is that too much to ask?"

"I promise, Mr. Taylor," Miranda said, surprising herself by giving him a hug. "Thanks for letting Elliot ride."

Starlight stretched his neck as far as he could over the stall door, nickering a greeting. Standing outside his stall, she pulled an apple from her coat pocket. With her pocket knife she began cutting off slices and feeding them to him.

"You look like you're doing fine. I guess that mean man didn't get much of that poison into you. It serves him right that it stuck into his own hind end."

"Miranda, did you notice his foot?" called Elliot as Mr. Taylor led Sunny to the hitching post near the tack shed.

"No, what?" she asked moving past Starlight's head to lean over the stall door. She saw that his cast had been removed. "Oh, Starlight, let me see!"

She went inside, quickly bent down, and grasped his back leg just above the fetlock. A blow to her back side sent her sprawling on her hands and knees.

Tears came quickly to her eyes as she realized that Starlight had intentionally swatted her with his head.

She heard Elliot giggle. "You should've seen that. His ears went back, and he knocked you right over."

"It's not funny, Elliot. He's never done anything like that to me before," Miranda exclaimed. "I just gave him a treat, and this is what I get."

"Oh, did you get hurt?" asked Elliot, seeing her tears. "I'm sorry I laughed. It didn't look as if he hurt you, or I wouldn't have."

"No. I'm not hurt at all. Just my feelings. I didn't expect it, that's all."

"Do you think he's getting mean?" asked Elliot.

"No, I just forgot to let him know what I was going to do. And maybe his leg is sore. I'll try again."

She patted Starlight's shoulder.

"Hey, boy, I'm going to look at your foot, okay?" Miranda made sure she had his full attention.

Moving her hand along his side and down his hip, she gently gripped his rear cannon and lifted. Starlight raised his foot for her. A jagged half-inch wide line of hairless scar tissue ran half way around his pastern just above his hoof. It was clean and dry.

"When was Dr. Talbot here?" Miranda asked, as she

eased his foot to the floor. "Did he say anything about the blood test?"

"He left just before I got home from school, but Grandfather told me about it. He said there was a trace of the poison in his blood, and it was the same thing that Queen had in hers. They're both going to be okay. Grandfather said we should exercise him today. He'll tell you what to do. Wait here; I'll go get him."

"Put a halter on him. It's starting to snow, so you can lead him around the indoor arena a few times," said Mr. Taylor from the doorway. "At the first sign of a limp, though, I want you to stop."

As Miranda led Starlight to the arena, Mr. Taylor, Elliot, and Laurie came along.

"Mr. Taylor, have you heard anything about Martin Hicks?"

"Yeah, I checked with the sheriff yesterday. He's going to be okay. Apparently he only got a little of the curare in his system, but they had to do surgery on his shoulder."

"What's going to happen to him? When's he getting out of the hospital?" Miranda stopped and faced Mr. Taylor. She was horrified that he might be free to come back and finish what he'd started.

"He'll be transported to Ohio the minute he's released. The sheriff found out he escaped from a mental institution back there. He's insane, Miranda. They say it's from some drug he overdosed on as a kid. He almost died then, but they saved him. It was too late to save his mind, though."

"How did he get the curare stuff? It must have taken a lot for both horses." Miranda had overheard Grandpa ask Grandma that question the night before.

"He stole it from a hospital pharmacy where he worked for awhile," Mr. Taylor explained.

"Why didn't they arrest him?"

"They've been looking for him. In fact he left a string of robberies across the country, mostly drugs. But he always kept just one step ahead of the law."

"Why did he take curare? It would have killed him if he'd taken it."

"I don't know what he originally intended to do with it, but after I fired him, he must have decided to get even with both of us by killing the horses."

"How stupid!" Miranda said.

"No one ever accused him of being smart. Though he could act pretty sane. He had me and a lot of other people fooled for awhile. And he knew drugs."

"I hope they keep him locked up good this time. I guess I should be glad he didn't die," Miranda said, turning toward the arena again.

"Well, I suppose someone bigger than you and me makes those decisions. It's a good thing, too," Mr. Taylor assured her, patting her back. "Don't worry. You've seen the last of Martin Hicks."

As Miranda stepped into the arena, what she saw stopped her in her tracks.

"Hip, hip, hooray, the winners of the day!" cried a crowd in unison. Startled, Starlight jumped back, pulling Miranda off her feet.

"Are you all right?" asked Laurie as Miranda got up.

"What's going on in there?" Miranda demanded.

"Go on in and see," Laurie said with a smile.

Starlight followed warily, his ears pricked forward and his head high. Miranda was just as cautious as she surveyed the inside of the arena. Balloons and banners decorated the hurdles and barrels that were still set up from the last day of practice before the Winter Fair. In a wheel chair draped with blue and white streamers, Higgins came to meet her. He held a sign that said, "Miranda and Starlight, our champions!"

"Higgins, what does this mean?" asked Miranda, leaning to hug him.

"It was Christopher's idea, but we all thought it was a good one. We're celebrating your life and Starlight's courage. Or is it your courage and Starlight's life? Anyway, this is to let you know we're glad you're both alive."

"Chris! You said you were going to Dillon today," Miranda accused.

"I had to have some excuse to get here ahead of you," Chris laughed. "You didn't get a chance to win your blue ribbon at the fair, and I know you would've. I thought you should have one, and Queen has plenty to spare."

He went to Starlight and placed one of Queen's ribbons around his neck.

"Hey, Kiddo!" Miranda's heart skipped a beat. She couldn't believe what she was hearing.

She spun around, her eyes and mouth wide open, and found herself staring into her mother's deep blue eyes. She rushed into her mother's open arms.

"Mom, what are you doing here? How did you get here? When did you come?"

"Slow down, sweetie. I couldn't believe my eyes when I turned on the TV yesterday morning. There you were on national news. Just a short clip. I thought I must be mistaken, so I looked up the Butte paper on the internet. There was your picture on the front page with the headline, 'Local Schoolgirl and Horse Capture Fugitive.' When I checked the answering machine later, there was a message from Mom, telling me all about it. Adam told me you thought someone was out to get your horse, but no one would believe you."

"Adam? He was there?"

"Yes, he brought a copy of the letter, so he could tell me about Barry," Mom paused to clear her throat and wipe away a tear. "We'll have to talk about that later. It's another reason I wanted to come. Luckily, I was able to get a standby ticket on the same flight as Adam. We flew together, and I learned even more about your father." Mom stroked her face and looked deep into her eyes.

Miranda snuggled into her mother's arms, and looked over her shoulder at the faces of people who had grown very important to her. Was it possible that only a few months ago she thought she had no friends?

"I'm reading the book you gave me. I really like it. We can read it together now, can't we?"

"You bet. We'll read every night. I have a week off before I have to fly back. If we finish it by then, and if you like it as much as I did, I'll get you the sequel," Mom said, hugging her again.

"Look, Miranda, do you see what you're horse is do-ing?" Laurie asked, laughing and pointing.

Miranda turned to see Starlight eating the cake that was set up on the platform at the end of the arena. He lifted his head as a groan from the audience turned to laughter.

"That's okay," Miranda said, running to him. "You're a hero, Starlight. Have all the cake you want."

Someone snapped a picture of them as she patted his neck and wiped white icing from his muzzle.

If you enjoyed *Starlight's Courage,* you won't want to miss the other five books about Miranda and Starlight. See information and order form on the following pages.

P. Lehkuhl

Most of our books are graced with illustrations by talented and prolific artist, Pat Lehmkuhl. Besides book illustrating, Pat freelances for *Simply Home,* where her original oil painting are reproduced on textile items. She also commissions portraiture, murals, still lifes, animals, and landscapes.

MORE QUALITY FICTION
FROM
RAVEN PUBLISHING, INC.

Look—and ask—for these titles in your local bookstore.

The Miranda and Starlight six book series
by Janet Muirhead Hill

Middle-grade fiction about the bond between two free-spirited creatures, a girl and a horse. This six book series for readers ages 8-14 tackles contemporary issues in an exciting drama that keeps readers turning the pages:

10-year-old Miranda Stevens lives with her grandparents on their Montana dairy farm while her mother seeks a career in Los Angeles. Miranda finds it hard to fit into a small school where all the other girls in her class are daughters of cattle ranchers and have horses of their own. When Miranda accepts a dare from the class bully, her troubles—and a deep and lasting love for a young stallion—begin.

When asked to make three wishes, Miranda answers; a best friend, a regular family, and a horse of her own. Throughout the six books of this award-winning series, Miranda and Starlight exhibit courage, loyalty and trust, as Miranda learns the value of honesty and friendship—and her wishes, one by one, come true in the process.

Grandma and Grandpa and even the old groom, Higgins, offer the impulsive Miranda a solid base of steadfast love and concern. From the strange mismatch of characters, an extended family unit is drawn together with Miranda at its center. Each member learns valuable lessons from the mistakes they make. It is a story of kids coming of age as they meet contemporary issues, and through trial and error, begin to find their own truths.

Fergus, the Soccer-Playing Colt by Dan A. Peterson

The witty, fast-paced account chronicles the adventures of a palomino colt who was bred to play polo but becomes a soccer goalkeeper, instead. As news of this wonder-colt spreads, he and the two boys who love him, Bobby and Ramon, are taken on a tour of the nation to promote soccer. Hearing of the famous colt, an unscrupulous rodeo stockman and his colorful sidekicks seek to capitalize on the colt's athletic ability. You'll laugh at Rumble and Reiterate as they plan and carry out a horsenapping—and reap the consequences.

Absaroka by Joan Bochmann

In this heartfelt drama of love, war, and the tenacity of the human spirit, young Matt Reed returns from Vietnam to the Wyoming ranch that has been in his family for three generations before him. Matt, who is struggling with the after-effects of war, is confronted with challenges of a changed world and a ranch in jeopardy. His attempts to solve the dilemma, show him the importance of overcoming pride to accept help from ranching neighbors, old friends, the Crow tribe, and even a herd of wild horses.

An Inmate's Daughter by Jan Walker

This middle-grade fiction, set in Tacoma, WA and at McNeil Island Corrections Center, shows just what it feels like to have a parent in prison. 13-year-old Jenna, who feels ostracized and isolated, struggles to find her identity and her place in society. When she jumps into Puget Sound to rescue a little girl, her mother is furious at her for drawing attention to the island where her dad is a prisoner. Jenna, who wants to be part of the school's multi-racial "in group" finds it hard not to break her mother's don't-tell rule. This engaging story reflects the reality faced by over 2 million American children with a parent in prison or jail. The children are doing time, too.

Danny's Dragon by Janet Muirhead Hill

Ten-year-old Danny's father went to war in Iraq and was killed in action. Danny struggles with the various stages of grief as he remembers good times with his father. With his vivid imagination, he turns Dragon, the horse his father gave him, into a means of escaping the reality he cannot accept. To add to his grief, financial problems caused by his father's death force Danny, his mother, and sister to leave their Montana ranch. Danny's struggle to understand himself, his family, and the world is compounded when he attends a Denver public school and comes face to face with the "enemy" — a boy from Iraq.

A Horse to Remember by Juliana Hutchings

After her family relocates to the small country town of Lewisberg, Tennessee, Hilary Thompson, who has lived and thrived in the city her whole life, feels as if her world has stopped turning. But when she begins working at the local stables owned by Susan Collins, she discovers Satan, a beautiful wild mustang stallion who belongs to Susan's rebellious son, Jeremy. Hilary immediately relates to Satan, who seems as lonely and out-of-place in his new surroundings as she is in hers. When Jeremy is unable to tame the horse, his mother threatens to sell him. Hilary embarks on a mission to tame him. But can a girl who knows nothing about horses tame an aggressive mustang? And will she be able to keep her efforts a secret? Encouraged by a new friendship and suffering the aggravation of a new rival, Hilary's determination to train Satan and become a champion increases. As her affection for the wild mustang grows, Hilary learns about horses, people, and the greatest lesson of all, love.

To order any of these books,
please contact:

Raven Publishing, Inc.

PO Box 2866, Norris, MT 59745

Phone 866-685-3545   Fax 406-685-3599
email: info@ravenpublishing.net

or

order online at:
www.ravenpublishing.net

Or use the convenient order form.

To order, send check or money order to:
Raven Publishing, Inc.
P.O. Box 2866, Norris, MT 59745
Add $2.00 shipping and handling
for one and $.50 for each additional book.

Name_____

Address_____

City_____State_____Zip_____

Quantity	Title	Price	Total
_____	**Miranda and Starlight, Revised Edition**	**$ 9.00**	_____
_____	**Starlight's Courage, Revised Edition**	**9.00**	_____
_____	**Starlight, Star Bright**	**9.00**	_____
_____	**Starlight's Shooting Star**	**9.00**	_____
_____	**Starlight Shines for Miranda**	**9.00**	_____
_____	**Starlight Comes Home**	**9.00**	_____
_____	**Fergus, The Soccer-Playing Colt**	**9.00**	_____
_____	**An Inmate's Daughter**	**9.00**	_____
_____	**Absaroka**	**10.00**	_____
_____	**Danny's Dragon**	**10.00**	_____
_____	**A Horse to Remember**	**10.00**	_____

Subtotal _____

Shipping _____

Total: _____